Shouting It Out

STORIES FROM CONTEMPORARY SCOTLAND

Edited by Tom Pow

Hodder & Stoughton

A MEMBER OF THE HODDER HEADLINE GROUP

ACKNOWLEDGEMENTS

All the stories in *Shouting It Out* were specially written for the book, although one of them, George Mackay Brown's "The Fight in 'The Plough and Ox'" has recently appeared in his collection *Winter Tales* (published by John Murray), and another, Liz Lochhead's "The Cure" has been broadcast by BBC Scotland.

The editor and publishers wish to thank all the authors who have contributed to *Shouting It Out* and to Gordon Jarvie who first saw its potential.

Orders : Please contact Bookpoint Ltd, 78 Milton Park, Abingdon, Oxon OX14 4TD. Telephone: (44) 01235 827720, Fax: (44) 01235 400454. Lines are open from 9 am - 6 pm Monday to Saturday, with a 24-hour message answering service. Email address: orders@bookpoint.co.uk

British Library Cataloguing in Publication Data
A catalogue record for this title is available from The British Library

ISBN 0 340 65501 1

First published 1995
Impression number   10 9 8 7 6 5 4
Year   2005 2004 2003 2002 2001 2000

Typeset by Transet Ltd, Coventry, Warwickshire.
Printed in Great Britain for Hodder & Stoughton Educational, a division of Hodder Headline Plc, 338 Euston Road, London NW1 3BH by Redwood Books, Trowbridge, Wiltshire.

CONTENTS

INTRODUCTION

The thinking behind this book is very simple: to bring Scottish writers and a (mainly) teenage audience together by commissioning authors to write stories especially for teenagers. Why should this be desirable?

There are many answers to that question but first among them must be that it is vitally important in what has been called the Age of Hollywood that all people wherever they are assert their own imaginative freedoms and value their own experiences. In every culture stories have had a central role in doing that. So we should tell our own stories; not simply tell them, but have them published and read by as wide an audience as possible. If you pay attention to something it responds and flourishes, and one of the remarkable things that has happened in Scotland in the last fifteen years or so is the number of novels and stories people are writing because there are publishing possibilities for them and a readership awaiting them.

However for many years most of the contemporary writing that appealed to teenagers and so found its way into schools came from outwith Scotland, mostly from the Northern England School of Realism, writers such as Stan Barstow, Bill Naughton and Barry Hines or from American writers such as Judy Blume and H.E. Hinton. Most of the Scottish writing that was available or suitable for schools came in anthologies of work culled from collections aimed primarily at adults. This meant that many of Scotland's most accomplished writers were not reaching a young audience and that young people in Scotland and elsewhere were unaware of the richness of modern Scottish writing. It is ironic that when recent research shows that babies at eight weeks old prefer the sound of their mother tongue to any other that many young people in Scotland could leave school without ever having heard their own voice, which in the case of Janet Paisley's story "Killer Mum", comes from Central Scotland: "Ah'll never live it doon. Ma Mum an Dad ur furst up oan the flair. Them an the couple they wur talkin tae. The Twist! That's sixties stuff. Yit baith ae them wur in their prams. Noo thur aff thur trolleys."

But it would be a mistake to emphasise the Scottishness of these stories at the expense of their other qualities, the perceptions of writers who are different ages and who live in very different surroundings. Alison Fell for example in "Our Lady of the Mammoths" shows just how elastic – or slippery – Scottishness can be with a story set in a Siberia she has created in part from memories of childhood holidays in the Highlands: "On the brow of the hill Valeria lay down in the snow and stared blankly at the sky. It was blue as glass and not a bird moved in it. Sasha knelt down beside her and rubbed her cold hands roughly, trying to warm them. 'Don't give in, Valya,' he pleaded. 'We're not finished yet!'"

Certainly the themes dealt with by all the writers are ones that are in no way unique to Scottish experience. Many focus on that moment of realisation of change or desire for change, whether asserted loudly as in Brian McCabe's "Shouting It Out", or quietly but firmly as in the ending of A. L. Kennedy's "The Park". Whatever, most of the stories agree that the emotions that lead to change are "Better Out Than In".

This is a book with stories to read, enjoy and reflect upon, but it is also a book about writing. Each writer introduces his or her story with some comments about their experience of writing and what he or she felt was important to say about the following story. For Alison Fell for example, "Writing is about exploring ... about *not knowing* where you're going, but having to take the trip all the same, for the pleasure and risk of it." For Janice Galloway, such risks are very real: "Because of the way I write, I'd have to set my subconscious loose and there was no telling what it would dredge up to the light of cold inspection. Simply I was scared it would hurt."

The stories in *Shouting It Out* were written with teenagers in mind, and they are the ones who'll be able to judge how successful the stories are. Together with the introductions though, I like to think the book constitutes the first part of a dialogue; the second part will come when you take up a pen and take some risks for yourself.

Tom Pow
Dumfries, May 1994

JANICE GALLOWAY

*I was born in Ayrshire, where I not only went to school but taught for ten years. I have written two novels (**The Trick is to Keep Breathing** and **Foreign Parts**) and one book of short stories (**Blood**) amongst other things. I didn't start writing till I was twenty-nine because it didn't occur, though I always loved reading. I keep doing it because it allows me to be my own boss and it forces me to think hard. I have one son and live in Glasgow.*

Writing for any particular audience or age-group is one thing I find very awkward. It makes me feel manipulative and self-conscious. But that wasn't the whole problem. After a lot of thinking, I realised I also found it very hard to think my way into "being a teenager" because so much of that period of my own life had been deeply disorientating. Between the ages of twelve and twenty, a lot of wildly traumatic stuff has the possibility of happening: the whole mine-field of boy/girl identities, sexuality as a real and pressing reality, defining a distinct self against parents and authority figures, discovering that other people talk about you alongside an awful knowledge that somehow it really does matter, learning more radically and tellingly that not all homes are like yours (a double-edged sword, that one), awareness of dispensibility, endings and leavings of all kinds as well as, if you're lucky, beginnings. And I remember feeling all of it like my nerves were on fire. So apart from all the more writerly reasons I could come up with for being unsure of the idea, there was this other, more telling thing. I was scared. Because of the way I write, I'd have to set my subconscious loose and there was no telling what it would dredge up to the light of cold inspection. Simply, I was scared it would hurt.

It did.
I wrote it anyway.

BOOKS BY JANICE GALLOWAY

The Trick is to Keep Breathing (Minerva)
Blood (Minerva)
Foreign Parts (Jonathan Cape)

Mary Moon and the Stars

Mary Moon peed the floor first day of school. She sat in the middle of a yellow puddle and cried while the rest of us kept clear. I don't know who finally went for the teacher but it wasn't me. After that she was called Mary-Moon-that-peed-the-floor, all joined up together like a red Indian name.

Mary Moon was as thin as a string, white-yellow hair hanging down her back in rats' tails. She had specs with elasticated legs and her socks sometimes didn't match. Her skin was see-through and she smelled like a cat's cushion. She sat next to George Dickie who kept nipping folk. There were always marks on her arms. My mother said she was a Poor Soul and told me to ask her round for her tea but I didn't. I suppose I was scared of the rings under her eyes, her fingernails always needing cut. I told myself she wouldn't come anyway and just didn't bother.

She disappeared before the end of primary three. One day she just wasn't there and the teacher told us she'd left. I didn't see her again for years, till I was in Secondary School. Then there she was on the road in front of me while I was walking to my granny's so it was Tuesday. I didn't say anything the first time in case it wasn't her. It wasn't as though we'd been friends or anything. I saw her again the next Tuesday. Same rats' tails only tied back now, the panda rings more definite. She was a lot taller and didn't have the specs any more but it was still Mary Moon. I didn't speak that time either. Maybe I was hoping it was a coincidence and it wouldn't happen again. Maybe I was saving myself from something, I don't know what. But when she was there again the third Tuesday running it was obvious I'd need to acknowledge her somehow. I shouted Hello because I didn't know what else to do and she stopped walking to look back at me, hard. I crossed over then and said, You're Mary Moon, only just managing not to add on the rest of it. She was embarrassed anyway.

You live round here then? I said.
She looked at the pavement, pushing back her hair with the long fingernails. We moved, she said.

Oh, I said. And that was us stuck again.

It was the first time I'd ever really spoken to her so it was bound to be awkward. Eventually I came out with, I don't live here either. I mean, I know you do but I don't. Stupid kind of thing to say but at least it was something. We were at my granny's hedge. I visit my granny on Tuesdays, I said and stopped. This is her place here.

Mary Moon stood looking into me for a full minute. One of her teeth was chipped. Then my granny rattled her knuckles on the window, and I knew she would be standing there, on the verge of opening the window and shouting to come in like I was five or something. I didn't want a showing up so I said cheerio fast and belted up the path.

Maybe see you again.

I only said it for something to say. She was still standing beside the hedge when I went in.

My granny was laying the table, setting cutlery.

That yin's moved in at the back of the scheme, she said.

She'd obviously been watching us from the window. I said nothing.

She breathed on the back of a spoon, polished it on her cardigan and looked right at me. The bad end.

Murray Street scheme had two ends. One was nice with flowers and things in the gardens: the other end had bombsites with giant dogs roaming like dinosaurs all over the place. That was the end my granny meant.

Just the lassie and her mother. Sorry looking article, all skin and bone. Disny get out her bed. The lassie takes the milk in when she comes back at night.

She could see across the house from the kitchen window, she said. I wasn't sure what was so terrible about leaving milk out on the step but there you go. Asking my granny questions about what she thought she meant was more trouble than it was worth.

All sorts up that Murray Street scheme, she said, shuffling plates. Tinks noo as well. Damt disgrace.

The next Tuesday I met Mary Moon at the school gate. She'd been waiting for me. I don't know how she found out what school

I went to and I didn't ask, just walked her down the road. She hardly spoke. At the end of Guthrie Brae she gave me a stick of chewing gum and ran like hell before I got the chance to say cheerio. Every Tuesday after that we walked together going down the Brae to Stevenson Street, to my granny's place at the back of Mary Moon's scheme. We liked the same things on telly and hated soaps. We both liked reading and hated PE. Over the weeks I found out her and her mum had moved about a lot. They'd lived in six houses and she'd been to five different schools. Now she was going to St Steven's because it was nearer the scheme. I didn't ask whether that meant she was a Catholic. Either it wasn't important or I assumed she didn't know. What I did say was that my mother worked there. She'd been a dinner lady at St Steven's ever since I was four and my dad died. Mary Moon looked at me hard again, then nodded as if she'd suspected all along.

A couple of days later my mother came in from work and said, I met your wee friend the day. I wasn't sure if she was trying to be funny. I looked at her but she just kept putting messages away while she was talking. Somebody had come up to her in the dinner queue and said she knew me. My mother had given her extra chips.

Needs feeding up, she said. Always did. It's Mary Moon, isn't it? How'd you not tell me?

I had to go out for a walk.

Mary Moon. The idea of Mary-Moon-that-peed-the-floor being my friend. I didn't know why I hadn't mentioned her either. She was just somebody I walked down the road with, somebody who wasn't..well..whatever the word is for a person who's unusual in the way Mary was. Abnormal, maybe. No, that wasn't the word. Undesirable. Mary Moon was an undesirable. It came back to me from primary school, from Mrs Drever who kept trying to offload pupils she didn't like onto the Remedial Department. If Mary Moon was undesirable and she was my friend, what did that make me? I knew it was going to be a long walk. I had a lot of thinking to do. I knew folk looked at her when she waited for me on Tuesdays, sometimes calling her names. The kind of names my granny called her and worse. Maybe they'd start calling me names as well. Then again you got called names for anything at that place, for being too thin or too fat or if folk didn't like your hairstyle for godsake, for being too soft or too clever or any damn thing. I thought about Mary, hearing the names and just holding her head up, watching for me coming. Sometimes, if you looked close, her eyes would be kind of runny by the time I showed up but she waited anyway. Nobody else had ever waited for me at the gate. I knew then I'd miss her if she didn't either. That decided it. Pathetic individuals who called folk names weren't going to tell me what to think. Folk that tried to do things like that weren't worth having. I decided for sure.

After that I started meeting up with Mary every Tuesday after I'd had my tea. We went for walks, saw the odd thing at the pictures, went down to the shows if there were any on. Not that I was daft about them but Mary liked the Waltzers. Mary loved Waltzers, just watching them: the lights and people laughing. Then we'd go to Mario's for a single fish between the two of us if I had money left. Other times we went to Woolworth's to look at the make-up or sat down the shore front, watching the water. We could watch the water for hours. Sometimes, sitting on the railing with the tide coming in, she'd point to things in the sky and tell me what they were called. The Seven Sisters, Pegasus, signs of the zodiac.

Look, she'd say. That bright one, low down. Over there, look. That's Venus. It's not a star at all but look at it. Look at it.

And her face would look different. I asked her how she knew all that stuff and she said her brother had had lots of books about space. They were hers now. I hadn't known about any brother.

Is he married or something? I asked her but he wasn't. He'd died. He'd got something called TB and he'd just died. He'd taught her chess as well but she wouldn't teach me. She didn't want to bring the board out the house in case she lost the bits. I said we could go to her house, but she said her mother wasn't well and they never had visitors. I didn't ask again. Come to think of it, I never even walked Mary back to her door. She always said cheerio at the end of the road then ran, as though she was scared to be late. Or she was running away from something. It never occurred to me to ask what.

My granny didn't like me being with her much.

You'll get beasts off that lassie if you're not careful, she said.

Don't you be spending money on her. Your mother works hard for that money.

I told her my mother liked Mary but it didn't help.

Damt disgrace, she said. I'll be telling her don't you worry.

And so she did. She and my mother had a big row about it. It finished up my mother told her I was old enough to choose my own friends and there was nothing wrong with Mary anyway. My granny was furious.

Lame ducks, she said. Canny help picking up lame ducks and orphans the two of you. Just land you with trouble. I tellt her the same about your father but she had to learn the hard way. Don't say you weren't warned.

I was furious as well but I didn't say. You don't sometimes, you just keep stuff to yourself. I ate my tea round there in silence for nearly a month. I don't know whether she got the message or not.

The last Tuesday was really cold. No snow but the road was hard when Mary met me at the school gate. We had to take toty wee steps to get to the bottom of the brae and even then, we had to hold onto the park railings, laughing and giggling. The puddles were solid and see-through with bits of coloured litter stuck inside, and the grass on the banking was crunchy. Mary had on buff coloured slingbacks and ankle socks. Her legs were scarlet. After my tea, it was even darker and colder. I remember she had this wee cardigan and jumper with no jacket, her hands raw. I gave her my gloves and she put them on, then chased me to the end of the street, slipping on the frozen tarmac. We went straight to Marios and sat in with two coffees all night, putting money in the juke box every so often to pay for our keep. The records were all ancient but it didn't matter. Mario's was warm, the windows steamy from the fryer and there were wee bits of tinsel up. I think Mario liked us.

You've not got no jacket, you, eh? he said, pointing at Mary. Can't not have no jacket in weather like this. Silly lassie.

And he gave her a loan of his. The arms nearly reached the floor. She wore it inside the cafe with the sleeves rolled back then gave it back before we went up the road. Apart from that, nothing marked that night out as different, nothing at all. We said cheerio and I watched her haring off round the corner, running. Always running. Then there was just me in the middle of the road, the streetlights like sparklers in the frost. You could see the stars for miles.

Next Tuesday I waited at the school gate till my hands were blue but Mary didn't come. I decided she must be sick or something and she'd had no way to let me know. She wasn't sick though. My granny put me right.

Some carry-on up that scheme the other night, she said, dishing up soup. Poliscar and the whole lot. The lassie's mother tried to do herself in.

I didn't know what she was talking about but my stomach was tight. I looked at my granny and she looked back.

Bottle of aspirins or something. Social Work were all round the doors, asking questions. They've taken her away, hen, the Social Work. They couldny let the lassie stay in that. Not with her mother that way. Folks are saying the house was filthy, no carpets, or nothing. There's just a cooker and an old bed settee left. And a chess board.

Her hands set out salt, pepper, slices of bread. The smell of the soup was making me feel sick.

Chess board, she said, shaking her head.

I sat and stared at the holes in the lace table-cover, thinking about Mary Moon running off round the corner, flakes of frost on her cardigan. And what happened was I got angry. I got angry at Mary, as if she'd done something behind my back, kept a big secret from me and known this would happen all along. But I also knew, of course I knew, she couldn't have. She'd been enjoying herself. Then she'd gone home. To what? Jesus. I pushed my plate away. My granny lifted her spoon and looked at me.

She'll be all right, she said. She'll manage. Now eat your soup.

Walking back that night was terrible. I didn't know if I'd ever see her again and I suspected I wouldn't. She didn't have my address or anything. I stood at the end of the Guthrie Brae and looked over to where her house had been, wondering why I'd never asked some things. But you don't. Some things you just don't push. At least she still had my gloves. Remembering that helped somehow. Not much, but it helped. Something fell on my face then and I looked up. Snow. It was snowing. I looked higher. There were no stars. None at all.

Five years later, getting near to Christmas, my mother came in from her work and dumped her bag on the table. I was just in in front of her, putting the kettle on to make us both a cup of tea when she said, You'll never guess who I saw down the Main Street.

I knew right away. For some reason I just knew.

Mary Moon, she said. I saw Mary Moon in Dockhead Street.

She was fatter, my mother said, boyfriend on her arm and a short skirt, an English accent when she spoke. If it hadn't been for the white-yellow hair, she'd never have recognised her. She'd moved to England, was working in a bank and engaged to be married. The two of them were just up for the day or so and she told my mother to say she was asking for me. I looked over. My mother was looking out the window.

Canny be more than nineteen, she was saying. But she's looking all right. She's looking fine.

She turned round then and looked at me.

I asked her if she wanted to come over.

I said nothing.

But don't be surprised if she doesn't hen. Don't be surprised if she doesn't.

I looked down at the teacups, knowing things. I knew really it had nothing to do with being busy. Mary Moon was doing ok. She didn't need reminders of before and I was part of before. I knew things about Mary she didn't want to know herself. I was sad about that but it was ok. If she didn't want to come, it was fair enough. Mary was doing the best she knew how. The cups were waiting. I lifted the carton and poured milk in.

I won't, I said. You want this tea, then?

She smiled and took the cup, cradling it between her hands. We can go Christmas shopping tomorrow if you like.

Fine, I said, smiling back. Fine. I'd like that.

So we did. I bought presents, cards with angels on the front and two rolls of wrapping paper. One was red and green squares filled with hearts, holly wreaths and snowflakes: the other, midnight blue, scattered with stars.

DUNCAN MCLEAN

I was born in 1964 in Fraserburgh on the north-east tip of Aberdeenshire. To begin with I was more interested in drawing than in writing. All the way through school I drew and painted cars and planes and cartoon characters. A favourite thing was to draw maps of imaginary countries. I'd go into great detail, showing all the roads and towns, all the lochs and mountains. I'd even imagine the kind of houses folks lived in, the clothes they wore, the food they ate.

Eventually, though, I had to admit that I wasn't a very good artist. I could imagine the people and places in my head okay, but when I tried to draw them, they usually came out wrong. So more and more I started writing instead of drawing: I made up stories and jokes and poems, even songs. I suppose I'm still doing that today. The difference is that instead of just writing to please myself and one or two friends, I try and write so that anyone at all can enjoy my stories.

Nowadays I live in a small town in Orkney. I write every morning, and when I've finished a story I post it off to a magazine editor or a book publisher down south. Sometimes the stories get rejected, but other times they are accepted for publication and I get paid. Usually folk get paid for doing things they don't want to do; I'm lucky that for a couple of years now I've been earning my living by doing work I love.

It doesn't feel like work when it's going well. It feels like me making up stories, just like I've always done.

I grew up in a fishing town, and now I live in another small port, so I've always been interested in boats and ships. I've been to sea in ferries of all sizes, in old fishing boats, and in friends' sailing dinghies, but most often I stand on the pier watching other folk sail away. Sometimes I follow them in my imagination, picture them fighting their way through storms or chugging across flat calms, hauling in nets of fish or dropping off scuba divers or lobster creels or oil-rig supplies. I suppose this story is one such imagining.

I know I'm not the only person to wonder about what goes on once the boat moves out of the safety of the harbour. One of my favourite story-writers, the American Jack London, wrote many tales about oyster-dredging and pirating off the coast of California. And the Scottish novelist Neil Gunn wrote a good book about herring-fishing called **The Silver Darlings***.*

When you're sailing out of sight of land, you're always aware of how big the sea is, and how small your boat is. There are no distractions: just you and two or three others on a lump of metal — and water, water, water as far as you can see. This always sets me thinking. In the story I imagine a boy who is also set thinking by being far away from land, far away from home. He thinks about things that are painful to him, and he doesn't really want the folk around him to see that he's hurting, so he keeps his mouth shut most of the time. I think a lot of us do that.

But some things can't be kept bottled up forever, and in the end maybe they really are "better out than in".

BOOKS BY DUNCAN MCLEAN

Bucket of Tongues (Minerva)
Blackden (Secker and Warburg)
Bunker Man (Jonathan Cape)

Better Out Than In

It was ten to midnight, the harbour was dark and quiet. The only sound was the flat black water slapping against the stone piers. But as David and Jock paused at the top of the ladder down to Jock's boat, there was a cough and the sound of trickling water. David looked and saw a figure standing at the low stern of the boat. It was Wattie the boatman, standing and pissing into the harbour.

Jock climbed down the ladder and jumped onto the deck, his boots clanging as he landed.

God's sake! said Wattie, and looked over his shoulder.

Aye man, said Jock, and opened the hatch down into the engine room.

Aye aye, said Wattie, turning and wiping his hands on the sides of his overalls. You're late.

We'll still catch it afore it turns, said Jock, going through the hatch. Davy here was asleep. We couldn't go without the crew!

Wattie looked up at David standing at the top of the ladder, seeming to see him there for the first time. Aye man, he said. So you're the extra hands the night then?

David was going to say aye, but just then there was a loud bang from the hatchway, immediately followed by a roaring as the engine came alive, and everything else was drowned out. David could feel the power of the engine dirling up through the stone pier into the soles of his feet.

Jock came up through the hatch and slid it closed behind him. I'll take her out, he said to Wattie. You stow away the hawsers and anything else loose: I reckon it'll be a bittie lumpy out there. He walked along past the cabin, climbed the ladder at the side of it, and opened the door into the wheelhouse, perched high on top of the boat, its windows level with the pier where David was standing. You cast off when Wattie gives you the word, he said. Okay?

Aye. David nodded, looked along at the hawsers looped around the bollards at each end of the boat.

And mind and jump on yourself! said Jock, grinning.

Aye. David walked along to the bollard at the stern, tested the heaviness of the thick rope hawser with his foot, and waited.

As long as they were in the lee of the mainland hills it was okay, but once they got out beyond the headland there was nothing between them and the wind, and the boat started rolling from side to side as well as the usual forwards and back rocking it made as it cut through the swells. Straight away David's guts started kirning, and his head seemed to be getting looser on his shoulders, wabbling about. But he didn't show anything, just braced his back against the wall of the wheelhouse and his feet against the rubber matting on the floor, and concentrated on what Jock and Wattie were talking about.

They say that the two lighthouses act as leading lights, said Jock. If you keep the headland and the Skerries in line as you leave, and hold that course, then you'll end up smacking your nose on the Stack.

Wattie looked out the back window of the wheelhouse. Better shift a few degrees to port then, he said.

Jock turned the big wooden wheel slightly. How's that?

Wattie looked out back again, and David followed his gaze. In the distance was the fast blinking beam of the Skerries lighthouse, and closer, a little off to one side, the slower pulsing light on the headland. As David watched, the two moved towards each other, till there was only one light in the darkness.

Hold her right there, said Wattie.

Jock moved the wheel again, then settled back in the big leather chair fixed in the middle of the floor. Right, we'll just stay like this for the next six hours and see if we end up on the Stack. He rested his feet on the spar across the centre of the wheel. Easy, eh, Davy? Bet they don't teach you this in navigation!

David shook his head. Not yet, anyroad.

Not yet! Jock chuckled.

The boat rolled far over to one side as a gust of wind hit, then it rolled back again. Everyone looked out the windows, but there was nothing to see, only the black water with lighter lines marking the tops of the swells, and the dark sky, almost as dark as the water, clouded over and without a glimpse of the stars.

Navigation classes? said Wattie after half a minute. Huh! Some things you only learn by doing them. Is that not right, Jock?

God aye.

Like women, eh Jock?

Well, you're the expert there, man! They both laughed.

I've been out on a boat loads of times, said David, then had to shut his mouth suddenly as the boat lurched away to one side and a wave of puke leapt up his throat. Beside him, Wattie shifted on the bench, and wiped his sleeve across his forehead.

I ken you have, laddie, said Jock.

Not for a wee while, right enough, said David, and then had to shut up again. He was beginning to sweat, he could feel it, although it wasn't hot in the wheelhouse. It was actually quite cold, and the sweat seeping out of him was cold too, and greenish. If it had been light enough to see. David was sure he would be seeping green sweat, cause that was what he was full of: green, slimy, watery ...

The boat rolled violently. Wattie rifted, then jumped to his feet, slid open the side window and stuck his head out, just in time for his mouth to explode with vomit. The sick blew back along the outside of the wheelhouse and spattered down onto the deck below.

David closed his eyes, tried to breathe evenly. It was hard, with the boat lurching and reeling all over the sea.

Wattie slid the window shut, and slumped back onto the bench beside David. Then he hawked, stood up, opened the window again, and spat out into the dark. He sat down.

Dear oh dear, said Jock. What a palaver.

It's a bugger, said Wattie. I'll tell you this: I reckon I'd be mate on one of the trawlers by now if it wasn't for this seasickness. Master, even!

Do you reckon? said Jock.

God aye. I'd been on them ever since I left the school, ken. And I was working my way up through the certificates. It was just a matter of time.

So what's the problem?

Wattie wiped his mouth with the back of his hand. The problem is, whenever there's more than a six-inch swell I start chucking my guts up! Every single bloody time! Unbelievable! And me out of a fishing family as well, going right back! Every single time I was out on the deep-sea trawlers I just felt like dying, I was that sick. He shook his head. Cause it gets that bad, David: you're so sick feeling that you reckon jumping over the side would be better than suffering it any longer!

Mmm, said David, not opening his mouth.

Jock cleared his throat loudly, looked over at Wattie.

The boat rolled and lurched, and spray splattered like sick against the windows of the wheelhouse.

The bigger the boat the worse the sickness, that's what I found, said Wattie. That's how I just have my own wee one these days, just go around the cliffs after the lobsters and that.

Well this isn't exactly the *Titanic*, is it? said Jock. What's wrong with you now?

Ach, it's this daft design: the wheelhouse stuck away up here like a bloody balancing act! It swings you about all over the place like a boat twice the size.

Jock nodded, looked over at David. She was a tug originally, he said. Actually the type of tug that shoves things about more than pulls them. That's why there's big blocks of rubber up front. And that's why the wheel's so high up, so we can get a good view of ... Davy, are you okay?

David got to his feet, swaying slightly as the boat moved under him. He reached for the door and opened it. I reckon I'll just get a breath of ... The wave of puke came surging up his throat and he leant out the door and spewed and spewed, sweetcorn and chewed-up pizza flying out before his eyes all over the deck and the ladder. Somebody was saying something behind him in the wheelhouse, but he didn't listen, he didn't care, he just kept on puking till there was nothing more to puke, and a little longer after that.

On one side of his head was the casing sticking up from the engine room. It shook and vibrated with the roaring of the massive engine below. The metal of the casing was hot, but that was good, cause the air and the floor were cold. The smell of grease and hot diesel wafting up wasn't so good. David tried to ignore it, he lay back and looked up at the row of portholes on the opposite wall of the cabin. It was light outside, but still rough going: one second the portholes would be showing nothing but white cloudy sky, the next the boat would roll and dark waves flecked with foam would be heaving past the glass. Sometimes, when the boat rolled very far over, the swells would smash against the portholes with a thumping sound, and David shut his eyes against the sting of the salt water that was surely about to come flooding over him.

But the glass held, and after a while David opened his eyes, pushed back the blankets, and got to his feet. He looked through the nearest porthole. There was nothing but sea and sky in sight, no sign of the Stack. He was glad he had woken in time. He went out of the cabin and along the side of it, holding onto the railings all the way. Waves smashed themselves against the side of the hull, sending spray and lumps of water up all over him, soaking his jeans. He climbed the ladder to the wheelhouse and opened the door.

Aye aye lad, said Jock, who was sitting on the bench, smoking. How are you feeling now then?

Okay, said David.

Alright for some! said Wattie, who was now at the wheel.

Jock laughed. The boatman here threw up twice more! Dear oh dear ...

Did you?

Aye! Terrible! Still, better out that in, that's what I always say.

How about you laddie, said Jock, dropping his fag to the floor and grinding it out. Were you okay down there?

David nodded. Aye, I had a fine sleep. He shrugged. I feel fine now.

Good, said Jock. Cause we'll need you soon. We should be getting sight of the Stack any minute.

We should've been getting sight of it half an hour ago! said Wattie.

Aye, well, maybe. With that wind blowing all night, I'm not surprised we're a bit behind. And we only just caught the tide, mind. Still. He took another cigarette out of the packet lying on the bench beside him. Keep your eyes peeled, Davy. He lit up.

David looked out the front window of the wheelhouse. The horizon tilted to the left, then to the right, then to the left again. He slowly moved his eyes across the whole of the sea in front of the boat, but there was no sign of land at all. After a couple of minutes looking he sat down on the bench beside Jock, and took a plastic bag from his jacket pocket. He held it out towards Wattie.

Want a sandwich?

Wattie grinned. Great! He stuck his hand in, pulled one out, and took a great bite of it. Hey, Captain, this is what you need, a galley slave! Food and refreshments on hand all hours of the day!

Jock chuckled, shook his head when he was offered the bag, kept on smoking.

I didn't make them, actually, said David, taking a sandwich out for himself. My mum did.

God, we should get her on board then! cried Wattie.

She doesn't like the sea. David took a bite. The second he felt the bread and cheese on his tongue a wave of something green came up through him, and he had to clench his teeth and screw his eyes shut tight. He swallowed hard, and kept it down.

He put the rest of the sandwich back in the bag, and the bag back in his pocket.

The Stack was nothing but a lump of rock, black rock white with bird shite. It was wedge shaped, with high cliffs at one end, and low crags and a couple wee inlets at the other. At the side of one of the inlets stood three figures, two big and one small, but they were almost hidden from David's view by the hundreds and thousands of birds that were flying from left to right, right to left, upwards, downwards, at all angles in between; they were diving into the water, bobbing about on the waves, taking off from the water in flurries, climbing, circling and landing once more.

The boat was sailing in a figure of eight a couple hundred metres offshore. It was impossible to go any closer because of the rocks lying under the surface and the strength of the wind. Jock was explaining all this to the folk on the Stack over the radio. Meanwhile Wattie was getting down the rubber dinghy that had been lashed to the roof of the cabin during the journey out. Jock told David to go and give him a hand.

They hauled the dinghy off the roof and shoved it over the side of the boat, after folding open and tying back the railings there. Wattie wrapped the dinghy's mooring rope to the hand rail, and said David should keep an eye on it while he went and got into his wetsuit.

The dinghy rose and fell on the waves, sometimes swinging in close so it dunted its nose on the side of the bigger boat, sometimes being carried away so the tether was stretched tight. When the rope tightened suddenly it sent spirks of water flying up into the air like shot from a catapult. The water stung David's skin where it hit him. He put his tongue out and ran it around his lips; it tasted salty.

Over by the inlet, one of the figures was waving. David didn't wave back, just watched the three folk through the storm of gulls, watched the swells rising and falling, watched the dinghy at the end of its tight-stretched tether. Then Wattie was at his side, carrying an outboard-motor.

Pull her in, Davy, he said, and wheeched the zipper of the wetsuit right up to his neck.

David hauled on the rope. Wattie, he said.

What?

Why do you wear one of those? Why not a life-jacket?

This has got built-in buoyancy, said Wattie. And it keeps you warm. The cold kills quicker than the drowning, usually.

The drowning kills quick enough though, eh?

Wattie looked at the dinghy being tossed about on the waves, then over the stretch of rough open sea to the rocky shoreline of the Stack. Let's change the subject, he said.

But the dinghy was right in by the boat now anyway, and within seconds Wattie had stepped to the gap in the railings, waited till it bobbed up almost level with the deck, and jumped on board. He landed on his hands and knees, and immediately crawled to the back of the dinghy and started fixing the motor in place there. Once he'd tightened the wingnuts, he gave several sharp tugs on the starter cord, and the outboard burst into life.

Okay Davy, cast off! he shouted over the high-pitched scream of the motor, and David unwound the tether rope from the railing and chucked it down onto the floor of the dinghy. Wattie opened the throttle, and the dinghy shot away over the waves, him crouched low in the bottom of it, spray and clods of water breaking over the bows.

David watched him go, then glanced up at the wheelhouse. Jock was leaning out of the side window, watching too. He noticed David looking at him, and said something.

What? said David.

You ken what to do?

Aye.

Careful then, laddie. This is the difficult bit. It's been a doddle up till now.

The first three trips Wattie made he was just carrying gear: rolled-up tents, long poles with nets attached, empty plastic drums that had held drinking water, a battered suitcase and several hold-alls. David's job was to wait at the gap in the railings and tie up the dinghy when Wattie threw the rope to him. Then he had to grab hold of the gear that Wattie had passed over and chuck it in through the cabin door. All the stuff was soaked with spray, and often it was hard to get a grip. A heavy metal box marked CAMERAS slipped out of David's grasp and would've fallen into the sea, if Wattie hadn't been standing right below and caught it. Soon David's back and the muscles in his arms were aching from bending over the side of the boat and lifting the heavy gear. But this was why he had been brought, so he worked on.

On the fourth trip Wattie took more boxes, and a man as well. The man had stubble on his chin, and scratches and cuts all over his hands. He didn't say anything as David pulled him on board, but straightaway he began helping with the boxes.

On the next trip, a girl about the same age as David, maybe a year older, came onto the boat, as well as a small gas stove and a bundle of sleeping bags tied with string. The girl watched the dinghy skid across the waves for a second, then disappeared inside the cabin. David could hear boxes and bags being hauled about in there, but didn't have the time to look in and see what she was doing; Wattie was already on his way back with the last man and the last few boxes of gear.

Within five minutes everybody was on board, and the men were helping Wattie lash the dinghy onto the roof of the cabin. Jock had already turned the nose of the boat away from the Stack, fired up the engines, and was driving her through the swells towards nothing but sea.

The girl's name was Rhona. She'd been camping on the Stack for a week with her dad and the other man. They'd been counting and ringing the birds that nested there. She said there were a quarter million of them: fulmars, gannets, puffins, cormorants, guillemots … David nodded.

You weren't on the boat when they dropped us off, said Rhona.

No, said David.

It was that two men and another man.

Aye. Wattie's brother. But he's having a baby this weekend. At least his wife is. So he didn't want to be away out here. They asked me instead.

Is the captain your dad then?

No.

Don't look at me like that, she said, I was only asking. She folded her arms and turned away from him, looked up at the far end of the cabin where she'd stowed all their gear. Her father and the other birdman were crammed into the wheelhouse talking and laughing with Wattie and Jock.

Have you ever been seasick? said David.

Rhona rolled her eyes.

My dad drowned, said David. He was dredging for clams with Jock and got swept overboard. His boots filled with water and the weight carried him down. They didn't find him for a week.

Rhona unfolded her arms, turned to face him again. Really?

David looked away for a second. Aye. Six months ago. This is the first time I've been at sea since then.

Rhona blinked. Were you not scared coming away out here on this old rust bucket?

He shrugged. What do you think? he said.

GEORGE MACKAY BROWN

*I read **The Wizard** as a boy in preference to Scott and Stevenson, which we were forced to read at school.*

The only subject I was good at, at school, was the weekly essay. I liked history too.

I enjoyed writing little verses and tales, to pass the time, but showed them to no one.

After university at Edinburgh, I thought I would have to become a teacher, but already I was managing to get a few stories and poems published; so I thought seriously of becoming a writer, at home in Orkney, which is full of history and legend.

Only read what you enjoy reading. Never write unless you enjoy it. That's the best advice I can offer.

I have lived in the small fishing town of Hamnavoe (Stromness) all my life, and so I know both the fishing folk and the farm folk who live all around.

The fishers and farmers are not always fighting, as in this story, though there may always be an ancestral rivalry, owing to their work in two distinct elements, land and sea.

In general they get on with each other very well.

But in this particular year, food was abundant in the fields, and scant in the ocean currents, and so the rivalry had a dangerous edge to it.

A beautiful girl brought matters to a head, like Helen of Troy with the Greeks and Trojans long ago.

BOOKS BY GEORGE MACKAY BROWN

Winter Tales (John Murray)
Vinland (HarperCollins)
Beside the Ocean of Time (Flamingo)
Sun's Net (Chambers)
Greenvoe (Longman)
Calendar of Love and Other Stories (Flamingo)
Andrina and Other Stories (Granada)
Masked Fisherman and Other Stories (Grafton Books)
Selected Poems (John Murray)
Wreck of the Archangel: Poems (John Murray)

The Fight in "The Plough and Ox"

I

The farmers in the parish were peaceable men, and they drank on market days in an ale-house, "The Plough and Ox", kept by a lady called Madge Brims.

The fishermen's pub was called "The Arctic Whaler". There the fishermen drank when they came in cold from the lobster-fishing.

The men from the farms — the ploughmen and the shepherds — got on quite well with the fishermen. They met and mingled on the Hamnavoe street at the weekends, and sometimes exchanged a few bantering words. Once or twice a fight threatened, when the young ones fell to arguing, mostly about girls; but then the older men would come between the spitters and snarlers, and patch things up, and there was rarely ill-feeling.

But the country men never darkened the door of "The Arctic Whaler", nor did the lobster-men stand outside the door of Madge Brim's, the wall of which was studded with horse shoes, or thought for one moment of going in there for a glass of Old Orkney whisky, price threepence.

The men from the land and the men from the sea segregated themselves strictly, when it came to refreshments at the end of a day's hard work.

In "The Arctic Whaler", you would hear talk of smuggled tobacco from a Dutch ship; whales; halibut so big they broke the nets; shipwrecks; seal-women.

There was none of that kind of talk in Mistress Brim's — it was all about horse and ox, the best way to train a sheepdog, oats and barley, whether it was better to grind one's own grain or to take it in a cart to the scoundrel of a miller. Often, of course, the young men spoke about the lasses. The bonniest lass in the parish that year was said to be Jenny of Furss, the one daughter of a very poor crofter called Sam Moofea of Furss. Sam was so poor he couldn't even afford to drink in Madge's place, where the ale was a penny the pewter mug. Sam Moorfea had to sit beside the fire at home and drink the ale he brewed himself, poured out for him by his beautiful daughter, Jenny.

"Oh but she's a right bonny lass, Jenny!" said Will Laird the blacksmith, who, by reason of his calling, always drank with the farm men. "I would like well to have Jenny take me a mug of buttermilk, every day when I stand wiping sweat from me between the forge and the anvil."

"No, Jenny deserves better than that," said John Greenay, whose father owned a big farm. "I can see Jenny with her arms full of sheaves at harvest-time and her long hair blowing brighter above them in the wind."

The young country men seemed to vie with each other, that summer, in praise of Jenny Moorfea. Their faces shone with joy and beer. The old men shook their heads in the hostelry, as much as to say, "*We* thought that way once, too, before the sweet-mouthed lasses we married began to nag and rage at us ..." They winked at each other, the old men. "Ah well, but they'll find out in time, the young fools that they are ..."

II

It so happened that Sam Moorfea had such a poor croft, and three young boys to feed, that he kept a small patched fishing boat on the beach, and fished inshore for haddocks whenever he had a moment to spare from ploughing and threshing. His wife was six years dead, and so Jenny did all the housework and brought up her three brothers well, and whenever her father caught a basket of fish, Jenny took them to Hamnavoe to sell to the housewives there.

And so, Jenny got to know the fishing folk well too. And that summer, when Jenny had arrived at her full beauty, some of the young fishermen looked at her, and they thought they had never in their lives seen such a lovely creature.

That first night, in "The Arctic Whaler", the young men's talk was all of Jenny of Furss. "My grandfather", said Tom Swanbister, "saw a mermaid on the kirk rocks and he was never done speaking about her beauty, but — poor old man — he died without setting eyes on Jenny Moorfea ..." "I'm saving up for a new boat," said Alec Houton. "I have twelve sovereigns now in the jar in my mother's cupboard. I would pour them singing into Jenny's hands for one kiss ..." Stephen Hoy said, "I'm going to call my new boat *Jenny*. I was going to call her the *Annie* after the lass next door, that I thought I might marry some day. But now I've settled for *Jenny*. I'll get good catches with the *Jenny*."

There was a young shy fisherman called Bertie Ness. At the mention of the name "Jenny", a look of purest joy came on his face. But he said nothing.

The old fishermen at the bar counter shook their hands and turned pitying looks on the young fishermen. They had thought things like that too, in their youth, and they were still poor men, and they were nagged and raged at when they came in from the west with half-empty baskets.

III

It happened that year, that there was a very good harvest in Orkney, the most bountiful for twenty years. Even the poor croft of Furss was studded with golden stooks.

It was far otherwise on the sea. From horizon to horizon, the sea was barren. It seemed that the lobsters had gone in their blue armour to fight in distant underseas wars. It seemed that haddock and cod had been drawn by that enchantress, the moon, to far-away trystings.

It was a very hard hungry summer along the waterfront of Hamnavoe.

Week after week the boats returned empty from the west, to the shrieking of gulls and the mewling of cats and — worse — the tongue-tempests of the women folk.

No wonder it drove the men, after sunset, to "The Arctic Whaler", where they sat silent and brooding for the most part.

One evening Stephen Hoy and Alec Houton quarrelled with each other in "The Arctic Whaler" as to which of their boats could sail further west. It began mildly enough, but soon they were snarling at each other. Other fishermen, young and old, joined in the dispute, voices were raised, old half-forgotten ancestral disputes were aired; it reached such a stage of anger that Walter Groat the landlord told them all to leave, get out, come back when they had some money to spend (for lately they had been sitting at the tables till midnight over one mug of thin beer, all they could afford).

Out they trooped, like sullen churlish chidden dogs. The old men went home to their many-worded wives. The young men drifted by twos and threes along the street. At last they found themselves outside Madge Brims's hostelry. Inside, merry rustic voices were raised. Tomorrow was Harvest Home; they were getting into good voice for it.

The young fishermen did a thing never heard of before, they entered the tavern of the hill-men, the farmers, the shepherds.

A sudden silence fell. It was as if a troop of wretched penniless outcast beachcombers had trooped up from the shore, bringing the coldness of the ebb with them — and that was pretty much the way things stood that night, in fact, with the fishermen.

But soon the country men returned to their drams and their stories and their loud bothy songs.

One or two went so far as to walk across to where the bitter fishermen stood against the wall and give them a welcome. Will the blacksmith offered to buy them all a dram. "You look that miserable," he said.

The fishermen looked at him coldly.

"Can I do anything for you gentlemen?" said Madge Brims to the young men from the salt piers. They answered her never a word.

From then on, the boys from the farms, the crofts, and the sheepfolds ignored those boors of fishermen.

They began to talk about girls. It was the high mark of every discussion or debate or flyting or boasting in Madge Brims's hostelry — it was inevitable — and it ended up with praise of bonny lasses.

At last John Greenay, son and heir of the wealthiest farmer in the parish, his face flushed like sunset with whisky, said, "We all know fine who is the bonniest lass hereabouts, and that's Jenny Moorfea of Furss. And now I'm going to tell you men something — I'm going to marry Jenny in October. I'm going to take her home to Netherquoy. She'll be mistress there, some day."

Hardly was the last boastful word out of his mouth than it was silenced by the impact of a pewter mug. The mug had been seized from the table by Stephen Hoy the fisherman and hurled with full force.

And at the same time Alec Houton yelled "You yokel! You dung-spreader! Jenny Moorfea is coming to our pier to be my wife!"

A trickle of blood came from John Greenay's split lip. The pewter mug rolled about on the flagstone floor, clattering. That was the only sound to be heard for fully five seconds.

Then the young farm men leapt to the defence of their companion. They didn't like John Greenay all that much — he boasted overmuch about his gear and goods — and besides, they loved Jenny Moorfea more than he did (or so they supposed). But those young fishermen had challenged and insulted the whole race of farmers.

It was the worst fight ever known in a Hamnavoe hostelry since the days of the whaling men a century before. There was a flinging and thudding of fists — there were shouts of rage, contempt, fear, and pain — glasses splintered against the wall — heavy pewter mugs rang like armour on the stone floor — noses were broken, eyes looked like thunder clouds. Will Laird the blacksmith spat out a tooth. Hands closed about throats. There was the flash of a fishing knife. A table was knocked over and twelve glasses and mugs and a half-bottle of Old Man of Hoy whisky fell in ruins.

It was the knife-flash that finally unlocked the petrified mouth of Madge Brims. "Police!" she shouted from the open door of her hostelry. "Help! Murder! My walls are splashed with whisky and beer and blood!"

What did our heroes care about the law or about disturbance of the Queen's peace? The shouts of battle grew louder. It seemed, in fact, as if an element of joy had entered into the affray. Frankie Stenhouse the young shepherd kicked the sea knife out of Ronald the fisherman's hand. It was to be a fair fist-fight — no heart-stabbings, and no hangings for murder.

And still the wounded fighters (for not one of them now but had a broken nose or a thunder-loaded eye or a fractured jaw) melled bloodily on the floor, and raged louder against each other (with, it seemed to some, a mounting access of joy and delight).

Madge Brims had abandoned her tavern to go to the police station in the south-end of Hamnavoe, a mile away, to summon the solitary policeman, Constable Bunahill.

A cunning lazy rogue of a fisherman, Simon Readypenny, seized his chance when the battle was at its height to slip behind the counter and put a bottle of brandy into one sea pocket and a bottle of Jamaica into another. And he disappeared into the night, leaving the tumult and the shouting to the fools. (He was found, gray in the face, in a cave, the next morning.)

The tumult and the shouting! It had now reached such a pitch that it could be heard in the granite houses of the respectable merchants and magistrates at the back of the town; and the shopkeepers got out of their beds and double-locked their doors. Indeed, a Graemsay man claimed to have heard the din in his island across Hoy Sound.

Then, a sudden silence fell.

The combatants disengaged themselves. They got to their feet, they made some semblance of wiping the blood from their faces with their shirt sleeves. Will Laird the blacksmith took a splinter of a whisky glass out of his beard.

They would not look at each other. They shuffled their feet like naughty boys chidden by the headmaster.

They were all on their feet now, in the wrecked hostelry, except young Bertie Ness the fisherman, whose kneecap had been cracked by a random kick.

The warriors had become aware of a presence in the pub door. All the snarling heads had turned at once. Jenny Moorfea of Furss was standing there, looking lovelier than any of them had ever seen her before.

Jenny Moorfea pushed her way through the wounds and the dishevelment, and she knelt down beside Bertie Ness, the stricken one, the poorest of all the fishermen there, and she kissed him.

IV

That is all that needs to be said about the celebrated battle in Madge Brims's bar.

Six men — three from the farms, three from the fishing boats — appeared at the Burgh court the following week and were fined half-a-crown each for disturbing the peace.

Then all six of them went from the courthouse into a neutral bar and pledged each other like battle-scarred comrades.

The following April, Jenny and Bertie Ness were married in the kirk.

They rented a little house at the end of a stone pier. Bertie Ness went to the fishing, to begin with, with Stephen Hoy in his new boat, the *Annie*.

They had such good fishing that summer, and for the two succeeding summers, that Bertie was able to buy a second-hand fishing boat for himself, the *Madge Brims* and also to buy their cottage.

Now they have three children, and the two boys are as winsome as their mother, and the youngest — the daughter — is a delight to all the folk that live along the waterfront.

BESS ROSS

I did not begin to write until I was forty-two years old. My children growing up coincided with major changes, both within myself and within my community. There, the old order that I had always known was passing, hastened by the oil industry in our midst. What my eyes had always seen, my whole self began to feel. It became important to me that I try to put down on paper something of the people and the place that shaped me, so that others might hear the voice of Easter Ross.

There are certain issues which lie very close to my heart. People and how they relate to one another head the list. I grew up in a place and in a time when there was no age gap between us and our grandparents' generation. In that, we were very fortunate. To some extent that still exists today although the village now is unrecognisable to what it once was through the influx of people from the south who came to work in the oil fabrication yards. This has had its benefits and its losses. What has gone, I think, is the warmth of knowing everyone and everyone knowing you. It was this change that brought me into writing in the first place — a way of life was passing and no one was doing anything about it. I wanted readers to hear the voice of Easter Ross, an unknown place to too many. For them the Highlands will be Inverness, the Cairngorms, the Western Isles. But there is so much more. All waiting to be written about.

Young people are the future. They will go forward in a different way, with all that today's world can teach them. It should be immensely exciting to be young today, but human nature being what it is there are things that get in the way. "The Bit About Growing" is about one or two of these impediments. What I hope it shows is that we must take the best from our past and go on into our future.

BOOKS BY BESS ROSS

A Bit of Crack and Car Culture (Balnain Books)
Those Other Times (Balnain Books)
A Writers' Ceilidh for Neil Gunn [contributor] (Balnain Books)

The Bit About Growing

"Hand that bit there up to me," The Grilse pointed to the pile of driftwood lying stacked in the corner of his shed. It was the back end of the year and he was working on his boat. He had a mind to have her down in the spring.

Neil looked at the heap. He hadn't a clue which piece the worn, bent finger was pointing to.

"Is it this bit?" he chanced and handed a stout board to the old man.

"Ay, that one," he took the wood from Neil. "Come here and hold it for me." He placed the plank on the horsey*, lifted his saw from the bench. The veins on the backs of his hands were a network of knotted rope. Neil pressed down hard on the wood with both hands, ensuring that it did not slip.

"Ay, like that. Keep her steady." The saw whistled and wobbled as it tore through the soft bleached wood.

Neil watched as the old man walked over to his boat, measured the cut wood for size. He was glad to be away from his house; there was always some bawling going on. Between Jo and his mother mostly. Or Jo and his father. Like today.

Jo had risen late, no one was allowed to open their mouths the mood he was in. The usual morning-after story. He turned off whatever obscure programme their father had been staring at and fed his Schwarzenegger tape into the video. And that was when hell broke out. It ended with Jo slamming from the house, doing his best to take the door with him, and shattering its glass in the process. When Neil left the house some minutes later Jo was sitting in the greenhouse glowering at the sad geraniums, his foot tormenting the cat.

"Jo says he's going to Australia," Neil spoke to The Grilse's back.

"Hm," The Grilse straightened, turned from his joinery to face Neil. "The wandering ones. That's what they used to call us. That's Jo I'm thinking. This bit's no use." He walked back to the woodpile, tossed the discarded wood on the top then began raking

---

* horsey — a wooden trestle used in sawing wood

through it for a more suitable piece. Neil stood in the sawdust and watched him.

"His feet's itchy." He found what he was looking for and Neil's eyes followed him back to the boat. He walked slowly, his feet dragging on the shed floor. It was as if an invisible wire was stretched tight between his forehead and his toes forcing his head and shoulders down, restricting his footsteps.

"My mother says she's putting the flag up when he goes."

"Ach, that's your mother's tongue speaking. If I know your mother she'll have the pipe band out for him when he comes home. Catch that other bit for me like a good fellow, the bit we had," and Neil hurried to obey.

"Myself was sixteen when I left home for the first time," The Grilse spoke through a mouthful of nails. "The first time I went anywhere it was to Glasgow to get a ship."

"What, you were only here till then?"

"Different days, Neil boy." He tapped a nail home. "I went into the town once before that, walked in and walked out. Twelve miles each time. I had to go for the doctor for Old Mailey's teeth. The doctor pulled teeth in them days, there wasn't a dentist in it."

Neil found it hard to imagine what it would be like growing up in the village when The Grilse was young. Never going anywhere. He'd been to Orkney with the school in second year. Last year they went to France, in primary they went to London, visited the houses of Parliament, met their MP and were on *Jim'll Fix It*. His Mam taped that; they still had it.

"It was, as you might say, a rude awakening," The Grilse's voice brought him back.

"I think my mother's worried about Jo."

"Surely she is, she's his mother. Are you keeping that right?"

Neil readjusted his hold on the plank. The Grilse's shed was filled with sea things. Lobster pots lay about in various stages of disrepair, dark-green glass floats rolled on the bench and caught the light from the window; his driftwood took up every corner, and then there was rope. Of every thickness. Blue rope, orange rope, white rope, dark-brown ropey rope, which smelled of oil and the sea. In the middle of all this lay his boat, her keel in the air, a gaping hole in her side exposing her bones.

"Tell your mother that I'm telling her she's no to be worrying about Jo. Jo's alright. He'll take care of himself. Yourself'll miss him though, I'm thinking," and the look he gave Neil was keen.

"Not me. I hate all the fighting."

"Fighting! What's fighting? Is that no families?" and he took hold of Neil's end. His aim was still sure, he didn't miss a nail once.

"I better be going now. My dinner'll be ready."

"Right you are then. Will you come back?" He didn't turn from his work.

"Ay, okay," and Neil walked away from the ramshackle old shed, made out of wood and corrugated tin with a house window in the side. The tap-tap tapping of The Grilse's hammer followed him.

Peace had broken out by the time Neil returned home. As he put his head in the door only the disembodied sounds of the television set met him. Jo was back, sitting on the settee, his back straight. Too straight. His face looked softer after the fight, not quite so girny. His hair was beginning to grow back in. Two weeks before he'd had what was left removed for a double vodka bet. Some guys could look really hard cases with a skinhead haircut. Jo only succeeded in looking vulnerable.

"Where were you anyway, as if I need to ask?" he barked at Neil. There was nothing soft about his tone.

"If you know so much why are you asking then?" Neil threw himself down into an armchair, retrieved *The Beano* from beneath its cushion.

"Don't start," their father said.

"What stuff's The Grilse filling your head with now?" Jo carried on, his long legs stretched before him waiting to trip somebody.

"Nothing." Neil's head was in his comic.

"Ay, right enough, that's about the size of it," and Jo's left foot shot out to hook *The Beano* from Neil's hands.

Their father sighed loudly and threw them a heavy look.

Neil picked up his comic and went back to his reading.

"You listen to all that guff," Jo needled.

"It is not guff." Neil's eyes never strayed from the page: "He knows plenty."

"He's living in another century. 'I remember when I was your age ...'" Jo affected a thin shaky voice. "What does he know about anything anyway, old geek?" and his left foot began to nark at Neil's right ankle.

"He knows," Neil said, moving his feet. "Why do you think he left here when he was sixteen?" His voice was ringing, colour flushed his face.

"Where did he go to? To Inverness?" Jo scoffed.

"Well, smart Alec if you want to know, he left to join the navy. He saw everywhere."

"Who? Him? That old shape? Is that true?" Jo turned to his father.

"I don't know," his father said. "Yes, I think so."

"And I bet he didn't make as big a noise as you about going," Neil said and he drove a vicious kick at Jo's ankle. "Lay off, will you. Get a life."

"Cut it, the pair of you," their father shouted.

"What's The Grilse's real name anyway?" Jo asked him some minutes later when all was quiet once more.

"I don't know. John Mackay I think. The same as yourself. He's related to us somewhere. Ask your mam. She'll know."

Jo pressed his lips together and thought on that. The old guy!

"And you can get that homework of yours done," their father shouted at Neil, his concentration on the television momentarily broken. "Everything left until the last minute as usual. Do you want to end up nowhere too?"

"He's going to end up there anyway," Jo's laugh was derisory. "What's in this place for anyone. In this country? Zilch!" He was up on his soapbox again.

An indistinguishable mumble floated through the open door from the kitchen as their mother fought and lost in the battle of the water taps and the television set.

"Just because you mucked things up." Neil kept his head down and his grip firm.

"Who mucked it up?" Jo demanded. "I could be anything."

"Ay, but your problem, Jo, is you don't want to be anything. You make me sick. All I ever heard, all my life, was how clever you were and how couldn't I be like you? Now look at you! Five Highers and a heap of 'Standard' grades and all you do is drift around with that lot."

Neil was edging it and he knew it. He cleared his feet well away from Jo's firing line, tucked his head into his shoulders.

"Ay, ay, we all know where you'd be. Circumnavigating the globe like Vasco da Gama."

"One thing I wouldn't be and that's stuck in a shed all day."

In the silence that followed Neil heard only his own words ringing. Jo's face had fallen in on him, his lower lip sagged. No one had to tell him anything about standing on concrete all day cutting steel, feet crying, choked with the fumes from the paint shop. On the back shift never seeing the summer nights, in winter the stars. And not being able to find a sleep pattern. Under the stubble haircut he looked about four years old.

"Other people go to university, but not you, never you. You're so special of course." Neil wouldn't leave it.

"University! University. That's all I ever hear. From everybody. You can't move in this place without someone going on at you. 'You're still here, Jo. I thought you'd be off to the university by now.' Is university the world?" The walls were rocking to the volume of his voice. "I'm never going to want what they have. People telling me how to think. Will university make me play for The Washington Redskins? Will university show me where the universe ends? Just quit it, will you?" and he leapt for the door. The house held its breath as it waited for the walls to come crashing down.

"I'm getting out of here if it's the last thing I do," he announced after one of his weekends. At nineteen his life was going nowhere, and he was beginning to realise it.

"What am I meant to do? Sit in at night with my mammy and my daddy. I'm sick of driving about on my own looking for something happening. The only thing that's happening is me, racing the Thurso train. I'm out of it.'

That was when Australia came up. It was easier than the States, you didn't need a permit. You could go out on a year's holiday visa. That was for him. The States — one day, he said.

"Promises, promises," they all said.

"You'll be sorry," Jo shouted.

That's when his mother mentioned the flag. "As a matter of fact I'll likely raise the flag of every country if I can find them," she added.

"Ha," Jo said, making his usual exit.

*

The Grilse's breath came from him in short sharp gasps. He struggled for it, his chest felt as tight as a drum. He raked among nails in an old syrup tin, selected a few of the kind he was looking for.

"You'll soon have her finished," Neil spoke from the open door of the shed. He looked at the old man's repair. It wasn't very good. He'd used differing thicknesses of wood on the hole. And they were nailed on squint. The ends of some of his boards were torn where he'd snapped them with his foot. New wood was nailed on to old.

"Ay, a coat of tar over that and she'll be sound. As tight as a kettle. What do you say?" and he stood beside Neil to assess his work.

"Ay," Neil said. "No bad."

"I'll paint her later. Mary'll chase me if she'll find me even looking at paint with this chest."

"This blue here," he walked over to the bench, clapped a hand to a large tin, "and this white." He reached far back on the bench and pulled the white forward to sit beside the blue. "I'll do that later, if all's well," and he stood that way awhile, stooped over the workbench, his hands cupping the two tins of paint.

"I don't know, my chest's that tight," he spoke as if to himself as he shuffled over to the broken chair, lowered himself carefully on to it, his claw hand clasping his sharp knees. He tried to clear something from his throat but could not.

"I hope you're no going to that place," he said to Neil when he'd given up on whatever was obstructing his gullet.

"Eh? What?" Neil was sitting on an upended lobster pot, staring through the open door to the shore.

"When I was over at the shop. Getting the rolls and the newspaper. Two men were talking," he spoke between the gasps. "There's a house in this village. Boys are going in to it. They're at the drugs," he wheezed. There was nothing wrong with his ears.

"Well, you needn't be looking at me," Neil flared, his face as red as his hair.

"I hope not."

"Well you can hope, because I don't. Honest. I'd be too scared anyway."

"And what about Jo?"

"Are you wise? Jo would never touch anything. He even hates fags. I know some of those boys. Two are in my year. Deadbeats!"

and Neil was back to studying rock and shore.

"Dirty things!" The Grilse found what was lying in his chest, spat it on the floor.

"Well, you needn't look at me," Neil repeated and the toe of his right trainer made patterns in the stour.

"Bad things," the old man went on as if Neil hadn't spoken.

"Tell me something I don't know," Neil said. The Grilse could be funny when he liked, Jo wasn't all wrong there.

"You'll be thinking that I'm an old gowk." Neil jumped at the words. The old fellow could see inside him!

"No, I'm not. I don't." He erased the patterns, began on new ones.

"I had all that thrown at me when I was not much above your own age. And I didn't have the comfort of my home at my back. Nothing new there."

"Did you ever try anything?" Neil stopped his drawing, looked closely at the old man.

"No sir! Never!" He lapsed into quietness and Neil thought that was the end of it.

"What's in them? Now, ask yourself that?" and he thrust a bony forefinger Neil's way.

Neil shrugged his shoulders. "I don't know."

"No more do I. But whatever it is that's in them, it can't do anyone any good. That you may be sure of."

Neil said nothing to this. There was no point. The Grilse was off. If his shortness of breath wouldn't stop him then neither would anything that Neil might say.

"How old would you say that I am? Look at me now," and the voice was strong enough.

"I don't know," Neil said again, not wanting to risk offending him by saying something foolish.

"If all's well I'll be eighty-five years on the tenth of January. And the more that I know, the less I know, if you know what I mean."

Neil didn't. He hadn't a clue.

"But one thing I have learned and it's this. Inside every one of us is everything that we'll ever need. If we're lucky enough to have our health. All inside us here, Neil," and he tapped his spare chest with a forefinger. "Look at yourself now, bonnie with it too. Just like myself," and he cackled like a hen, clapped a tatoo on his knees.

Oh ay, Neil thought, I wish. A head like a coconut, a lump of steel in my mouth and now spots.

"Don't ever tamper with what'll harm you," the old man was serious again. "Look at me now. Are you hearing what I'm saying to you?"

Neil looked at the opal eyes. He had to force himself not to burst out laughing at the fierce old face looking back at him.

"It's easy enough to die. We all do sometime. Anyone can do it. But how we live, Neil boy. That's a different story. Are you hearing now?"

"Ay," Neil said, fiddling with the collar of his jacket. Cripes, the old fellow was getting awful heavy.

"Do you have a girl in that school of yours?" he asked, changing tack.

"No chance," Neil's face was a beetroot. He squirmed on the lobster pot as he felt the embarrassment take him.

"And what about Jo? Is he courting?"

"Him? Never! There's no one perfect enough for him. There's always girls on the phone but he can't be bothered. He says he's looking for someone like himself."

The Grilse opened his mouth in a wide gummy smile, shook his head. "I'm thinking he's going to have some search then. But mind," the smile slipped from him, "she'll be a very special lassie when he finds her."

"There's no such person. That's what my mam says. Not in the whole world. Can't be, she says. Imagine a female Jo. Doc Martens, a bad attitude and a bald head."

"Like myself," The Grilse chipped in.

"Ugh!" Neil's hands went to his throat, he pretended to faint from the thought. And the tin walls of The Grilse's shed reverberated to their wild laughter.

"Mind you, we saw all kinds in the navy. Ach, you saw everything. When I was not much older than yourself is. There was nothing in it for us then but to go to the sea. What else could we do? You got to know the fellows making the same trip. Sometimes you'd meet up with them in Montreal and Auckland and Valparaiso, Curaçao, places like that. Different places. You'd always meet someone you knew." The old voice softened, grew thin. "The best friend that I had when I was in the navy came from the

Island of Eriskay. A lot of the island men joined the fleet. Davy MacLennan his name was. Fine man. Oh yes."

Neil looked up at the old man's face. He didn't know what he saw written there. He looked away.

"Big, big fellow. Strong. Like a bull. He'd play anything on the mouth organ. His favourite was 'The Eriskay Love Lilt'. Do you know it?" and he began to croon something below his breath.

Neil shook his head. It was hard to tell whether he did or not. The Grilse's humming was practically soundless, totally tuneless.

"He'd play 'The Hilltown Fishers' to me. Now, you know that one?"

"Ay, my granda used to sing it. My mam still does."

"Good for her. We buried Davy in the South Pacific Sea. He got hit on the head with a hook from a crane. Ay," and he shook his head again, the way a dog does, as if he would shake the memory from him. He rose from the chair, walked over to the bench, began rearranging the tins of paint, gathering up and sorting the loose lying nails.

"How was he called The Grilse anyway?" Jo asked his father on the day that the village heard of the old man's passing. He had died four days into his eighty-sixth year. It was his lungs, they whispered in the shop. What had begun as 'flu carried him up to the cemetery.

"I'm not sure," his father said. "Ask your mam. She'll know."

"Well," Jo's mother told him, "Granda told me it was because he used to go out with the salmon-fishers when he was a wee bairn. And you know what a grilse is, a young salmon. He was at the salmon-fishing on and off all his life, whenever he came home from the sea. A carnhar★ like Granda was." She paused, looked to one, then the other. "Where's Neil?" she asked.

"Through in his room," they said.

Neil couldn't believe it. The Grilse had died awful quick. He said he was going to paint the boat. And he was dead. It wasn't fair. Neil screwed his eyes shut to try to stop the tears coming. He thumped his pillow as he fought for control. It just wasn't fair. Silly

★ carnhar — a salmon fisher

old fool, who did he think he was anyway? Dying just like that. Just going off without saying even one word. To anybody. "Anyone can die, anyone can die," Neil wanted to rip the words out of his head. His fists were pistons and his pillow was there. All the helplessness, the rawness, the lostness and the utter confusion that was choking him spewed from his fists. "Anyone can die, anyone can die." Big deal. Who cared? Neil flung himself across his bed and howled.

Later he was able to see clearly. He was walking along the shore one day, doing nothing, when he found he could look up at the shed without experiencing the red hot dagger in his chest. He wasn't sure what it was that he did feel, but whatever it was the cruel crippling pain was gone.

"It's how we live," he had said. And once, "To live is to grow. If we don't do that, what then, Neil boy? We'd be as well to be dead. Huh!"

Jo was in Sydney and they all missed him most terribly. Their days had a different shade of light without Jo. His father made a small noise about the reversed charge phone calls. But his mother didn't care. All she and Neil wanted was to hear Jo's voice. His father too. His mother swung between euphoria when Jo phoned or when a letter arrived from Australia to dark despair in between, convinced the whole of Australia was waiting solely to harm him.

Neil loved Jo. How could he ever have thought that he hated him? When he wasn't being aggravating and narky, Jo was ace. He wrote good long letters to Neil. He told him that the hardest thing that he had ever done was to get on the train at Inverness and not get straight back off again. And Sydney was a beautiful city. So clean, so much going on. All the time. And, oh Neil, you should see the nights.

In Sydney, eleven thousand miles from his home Jo would be doing his growing. As the time for his leaving had drawn closer and it dawned on his mother that he really was going, she nearly flipped. Yes, she did hear him right. He was going all that way on his own. And no, he didn't want any addresses. Of anyone. Unless she knew Crocodile Dundee. Being Jo he'd do it his way.

"He said that you were to have *The Puffin*," Mary, The Grilse's daughter, said to Neil as they left the house on the day of the funeral. Neil couldn't look at Mary's face; he left his mother and father to do the talking. Back then he didn't want to know about anything.

He stopped his walking, looked up at the shed again. It stood out from the neat concrete squares of its neighbours. The Grilse's shed was different. Like he himself had been different. Like Jo was. Jo like an old shed! Neil's grin was wide at the thought. He picked up a stone, pitched it far out into the waves. He must tell him that one when he wrote back.

As he looked at the sea Neil thought some more on The Grilse's bit about growing. The old guy wasn't all daft. No way. He searched around for a flat stone, of the right size, and sent it hopping through the rollers. Then he turned his back on the sea, walked up the beach and crossed the bank to The Grilse's house.

JANET PAISLEY

ME?: Write? Always. Invention — adventure games, daydreams, let's pretend we're ... wrote them down too — stories, poems, as soon as I could use a pencil. Why? Control probably. Children have none and I wanted a different world. Still do. Been publishing stories for fifteen years, poems for eight. Still writing.

KILLER MUM: Oldest son and I drive to the school Christmas concert. We blether as normal. He's sixteen — we have an easy-going adult relationship. I park, we get out and walk towards the building. Three steps and he stops. Mum, he says, what are you doing? Automatically, I make a ten-feet gap between us and ignore him. This has not happened before but I instinctively recognise he has reached the age when having parents is not the done thing. Striving for the effect, we arrive together, apart. I was not wearing a woolly hat — honest.

Children train their parents — but what if the parents won't be trained? That combination of fact and question created the story. Using the speaking voice puts the character fully in charge — they say the thing their way, not my way. The Scots is contemporary and Central, an unrecorded language translated from speech to page by a mix of traditional, phonetic and English spelling. To aid word recognition, glottal stops are not indicated in words like "buttons" and "mortified" though the speaker would drop the internal "t". Don't read it — speak it. It's a story for the Scottish voice.

BOOKS BY JANET PAISLEY

Alien Crop (Chapman)
Wild Fire (Taranis)
Biting through Skins and *Pegasus in Flight* (Rookbook)

Killer Mum

See ma Mum. She's a killer. Gaun doon the toon tae git new docs. Middle ae wintur. Whit's she weerin? A woolly hat. I kid you not. Knittit gloves an a woolly hat. An hus the cheek tae walk aside me doon the street. Come oan. Mean tae say. Wid your Mum dae that?

Ah try, ye know. Ah says "Mum, gaunnae gies a breck. See if ye waant tae impersonate a wifie auld enough tae be yer gran, gaunnae walk ower there a bit." Ah mean, it wis embarrassin. Fowk wur beginnin tae stare. Mum, she thinks it's funny. Starts tae laugh. An wha dae we meet? Stevie Wonder — real name's Lamont bit we caw him that because he's neat. Fourth year an a dream. Guess whit, the day o aw days, he stoaps tae speak. Whaur dae ah pit masell?

"Haw, Carol," he says. Ma insides swim aboot. Afore ah git ma mooth open, Mum comes ower. "You're Steven, aren't you?" she says, bool in her mooth like oan the phone. "I know your Mum. Are you going to the school disco? And your Mum and Dad?"

The Generation Gap this dance is cawed. Some smart Alec oan the staff thocht it wid be a guid idea tae git some money in. Fur patching up the minibus, ken. Efter yin ae them, auld Mr Keckle fae Chemistry, furgoat to open the school gates afore he backed it oot. Noo we suffer. An it's the nicht. Hence new docs. Wan thing. Ah'm swingin it fur aw it's worth. Take whit's gaun. Never ken when ye'll git the chance again.

Ah drag hur awa fae Stevie wha's went purple. Ramble oan aboot these neat wee toaps. Jist the thing fur discos. Help ma goad. Hoo dae ah keep it up? She's saying "Din't ye think the pink is awfy braw." Ah'm thinkin whaur'd the posh vice go, an pick the black.

Pushin ma luck, ah gie earrings a shoat. "Carol," she says. Means trouble that, gied yer name. Like suddenly thuv minded whit they cried ye way back when. The official "Ah um yer Mither" tone. "Carol, ye've goat three in that ear awready. Oney mair holes and ye'll huv a see-through boady." Intae exaggeration an aw. Ken ah'm wasting ma time by noo. Stull, done no bad. New toap, the docs an pre-shrunk jeans.

"Whit you weerin?" ah ask, hert in ma mooth, tryin tae soond aw innocent. She luks surprised. Ah drag hur in anither shoap. "Lit me pick." Wull she though? Ah haun hur a scrunched velvet hat an froak — purple cause she'll no weer black. Funereal, she ayewis says — an a bisque rope waistcoat. "An git they long bits ah tried oan, wi the buttons up ower yer ankles. Rave oan, Mum. Ma Dad'll think yer too hot tae trot." Aye, right. She laughs.

"Naw," she says. "Yer Dad'll think ah'm daft. See you, Carol, moanin aboot ma hat. See this," she waves the claes aboot, "ma great-*great* granny wid weer that." See next time ah'm in the Chemistry class, ah'll git that Keckle, leave the gas taps oan — chuck in a match.

So there we aw ur, in the hall. Me an aw ma pals. Fair mortified. Sumdy's hung a great big silver baw fae the ceilin. Peety they hudnae hung thersell up there an aw. Music's no bad. Kinna hauf an hauf. Naebdy's dancin an cause wur in the school, even the auld yins huv tae git thur engines gaun oan juice. Nae use. The DJ's knoackin his pan in tryin tae gie things a luft. Pits oan the Twist.

Ah'll never live it doon. Ma Mum an Dad ur furst up oan the flair. Them an the couple they wur talkin tae. The Twist! That's sixties stuff. Yit baith ae them wur in thur prams. Noo thur aff thur trolleys. Gein it laldy. Managin tae waggle airms an legs, miss every beat. Ye kin tell thur huvin a great time. Think thuv cracked it. Ma Dad wriggles doon tae his hunkers. Even ower the noise, ah hear his jints creak. Don't ask me hoo he gits back up. Ah'm aff. Awa oot the hall. A laughin stock, that's whit ah am. Thocht ma Dad hud better sense.

Oot in the corridur, ah'm near in tears. Atween the twa ae them, thuv feenished ma school career. Nut a shred ae street cred left, no efter the nicht. Hoo did ah git blessed wi parents quite sae dumb? An jist whin things couldnae be worse, worse comes. Stevie comes roon the coarner whaur ah've hid masell. He disnae luk well. Tries no tae see me bit he cannae miss. Noads. Comes an stauns aside me. No too close. Furst time ah've seen him no look share. Ye ken, withoot the famous cool.

"It's terrible," he says. Ah say aye. Inside ma heid ah'm thinkin whit ah need is fostered oot, taen intae care. Ah'm thinkin this is the last time they git oot oneywhere within a thousan miles ae whaur ah am. Ah'm wonderin if ye kin git done fur daen yer parents in. Strychnine, arsenic, cyanide — whit yin's maist painful, whit yin's slow an horrible — an agonisin lingerin daith. Me stickin peens in dolls. Ah see it aw.

Stevie says "Ah tried tae git them no tae come." Ah luk it him. "Ye whit?" He luks up it the ceilin, rolls his een. "Ma Mum an Dad. Furst oan the flair. Nae wey ah'll ever ..." Ah cannae lit him feenish. "Your Mum an Dad? Is that wha ...?" See that wurd, sheepish. Ah'd never seen him luk like that afore. No Stevie Wonder, real cool dude ae Braidwood High. Bit scratch him an he bleeds. Human efter aw. "Me an aw," ah tell him. "The ither twa's wi me. Bit no fur long. Kin ye divorce yer parents, richt enough?" He luks, an luks. An then licht dawns. He cheers up. Baith o us laugh. Laugh till wur sair.

He's chokin, tellin me, "Did ye see ma Dad sasheyin roon ma Mum? Thocht he'd goat his legs jammed sideyweys an wid keep gaun till he hut the waw."

"Ma Mum," ah'm hingin oan his airm, gaspin fur braith. "Ma Mum's leg wis in the air fur that long ah thocht it must be stuck up there." We laughed sae much it wis a while afore we realised wur staunin in the corridor aw by oorsells, hingin oantae yin anither. Yince we stoapped, we wur quite pally. Checked the Twist wis ower an done, an went back in, haudin hauns.

By noo the DJ'd goat a life, turnt oan the smoke machine, the sunfloor spoats, wis playin rave and techno stuff. Intae that. Me an Stevie. It wis guid. Time it feenished we're gaun oot. An item. Oh, ya beaut! See us abused weans, goattae stick thegither. We'll git oor ain back, bit.

Gittin in the motor, Mum says "Nice boy that." She's a killer, richt enough. Ah hud cloacked the luk she shoat tae Stevie's Mum. Oor dads baith lukt suspicious. Get aff. Wur fifteen. Havin fun. Wunner, should ah tell thum ah'm gaunnae be a brain surgeon? Pioneerin work. Transplants fur Twist fanatics. Start wi them.

BRIAN MCCABE

I was born in 1951, the youngest of four children. My father worked as a miner, my mother as a cook. I grew up in Bonnyrigg, King's Lynn and Falkirk, and began writing poetry shortly before leaving Falkirk High School in 1969. One of these poems won an award in the Scotsman's School Magazine Awards. As a student at Edinburgh University, I continued to develop my own writing and became involved in reading my work in public and organising readings for other writers. After leaving university I worked in a variety of jobs before becoming a self-employed freelance writer in 1980, when I was awarded a writer's bursary by the Scottish Arts Council. I live in Edinburgh with my family.

One of the most common questions I have been asked by readers — or listeners, after a public reading — is: "Did that story really happen?" or, "Was that based on personal experience?" It's not such an easy question to answer honestly and accurately, because, in my experience, most stories are a complicated mixture of elements drawn from life — sometimes, but not always, personal experience — and elements that are purely fictional or imaginative.

"Shouting It Out" is a good example of this. Some things in it are drawn from my memories of childhood and of being a teenager. I did go to the Saturday matinee as a child, cheered and drummed my feet, and I did see **The Time Machine** and had nightmares about those Morlocks. As a teenager, I did go with girlfriends to the pictures, and although I don't remember shouting things out during the film like the boy in the story, I do remember this happening quite often.

It was this idea which interested me most in the story and which became the most fictional or imaginative element for me — the idea that a teenager in a small town in Scotland might take it upon himself to be a kind of live film critic, satirising and poking fun at the romance, the glamour and the heroics the media feed him in the form of a movie. I could see possibilities of getting at a bigger theme, to do with how the media affect people's lives, by writing about this small incident. The idea of "shouting out" also opened up possibilities of writing about self-expression.

I was also interested in trying to capture what it feels like to be a teenager, to open up to another person for the first time, to fall in love without really understanding that this is what is happening. I wanted to get at the excitement of this but also the awkwardness and the terrible vulnerability of it. The boy in the story is having to make the difficult decision to ignore his friends' view of his girlfriend and have confidence in his own feelings for her.

The business of people trying to find out who they are, trying to define themselves, interests me, and I saw possibilities in this story of exploring this. That's what the "different kind of acting" is about — I remember my first relationships with girls being like that, as if we were "trying on" feelings, or playing a part in a film, except that there was no script, you had to make it up as you went along.

BOOKS BY BRIAN McCABE

One Atom to Another (Polygon)
The Lipstick Circus (Mainstream)
The Other McCoy (Mainstream/Penguin)
In a Dark Room with a Stranger (Hamish Hamilton/Penguin)

Shouting It Out

He could do it in the dark, with Christine there beside him, surrounded by everybody just sitting there watching the film, when the only sound was the soundtrack, so loud it was like somebody whispering in your ear. He knew how to wait for that moment when everybody was totally into the film, when nobody was coughing or giggling or whispering, when nobody was even eating popcorn. A moment like now, when there was just the eerie music and David Bowie taking his first step on the planet Earth. Without having to think about it, he shouted it out: "*Step we gaily on we go, heel for heel and toe for toe!*"

Christine thumped him on the chest and told him to shut up, but it had worked. Although she was embarrassed, she was laughing. Everybody was laughing — or it seemed like everybody. Really it was probably just a few folk here and there across the cinema, but in the darkness it felt like the whole cinema was laughing. Now it would be good to get them on the tail end of the laugh with something else, but already the usher's torch was looking for him among the seats and Christine was telling him to keep quiet. He huddled down in the seat as the beam of the usher's torch tried to find him.

"Keep it quiet along there!"

Christine punched him lightly on the arm. He liked it when she hit him. It felt so different from being punched by one of his pals. There was something very light and playful about it; it made him feel bigger and stronger than he was. He liked it when she touched him in any way at all. Even if she just touched his sleeve, it was like he could feel the touch on his skin. And although his friends said she was hackit, a dog, he liked her big brown eyes, her thick, dark hair, her wide mouth with the deep corners that twisted up so quickly into ´a smile — everything really except the nose. She didn't like her own nose either, and sometimes covered it a bit with her hand. At first her nose, and what his pals said about her, had really bothered him, but now he was getting to like being with her — they'd been going out together for nine weeks — and in a funny way he'd started to think her nose wasn't so bad. It made her

look foreign — Greek, Spanish or Italian. He liked the way
sometimes a little crease wrinkled the side of her nose when she
laughed. It suited her.

He watched the film for a while, but then, just as David Bowie
was arriving in the small town in the middle of nowhere in the
desert, he couldn't help himself. He had to shout it out: *"Excuse
me. Ah'm lookin for Mairi's weddin!"*

Laughter. But this time the usher's torch trapped him in its beam
and Christine hid her face behind his shoulder. He could feel her
shaking, shuddering against him as she held in her laughter.

"Right you — out!"

"Who? Me?"

He went through the routine of protesting his innocence until
the usher gave up and went away, with the warning that if there
was any more of it he'd be out. Christine hissed into his ear:
"What a red face! Can you not just watch the film like everybody
else?"

"Okay."

Like everybody else. He slumped forward in the chair, made his
mouth hang open and stared like a zombie at the screen.

Christine shook her head, thumped him on the arm and
laughed. That was what he liked about her, one of the things he
liked. He made her laugh.

He'd been coming to the same cinema since he was seven or
eight years old. He could remember a whole gang of them coming
to the Saturday matinee, sometimes bringing their roller skates to
skate down the aisle until they were thrown out. He remembered
buying cinnamon sticks at the chemist's and smoking them behind
the cinema before they went in. He remembered the old man with
the cap hanging over one eye who sold the Kia-ora. He was so old
and bent and wrinkled, they were scared to buy his juice. Climbing
over the seats, drumming your feet on the floor when the film
broke down, cheering when the cavalry arrived... Then there was
that really scary film called *The Time Machine* with the monsters
called Morlocks. They were big and blue and hairy, a bit like
gorillas, except they lived under the ground. Above the ground
was a kind of paradise. The people just played around all day and
wore futuristic clothes and ate exotic fruits, till they heard the

siren. When the siren sounded, they all froze and became like zombies, the zombies of paradise. They had this glazed look in their eyes as they walked, hypnotised, to the caves that led down into the underworld where the Morlocks waited for them, stirring the cauldrons, and guess what was for dinner... Although it seemed like a hoot now, the film had given him nightmares for weeks as a kid. He could remember checking in the wardrobe and under the bed at night, checking for Morlocks... And after his dad had come and put his light out and told him to get to sleep, he had sometimes shouted it out into the darkness of the room: "*Go away, Morlocks!*"

But in his dreams the darkness of the cinema had blurred with the underworld the Morlocks lived in, and the Morlocks were coming down the aisle with flaming torches in their paws, like wild ushers carrying wild torches, climbing over the backs of the seats, and the ugly old man who sold the Kia-ora had turned into a Morlock too, although the funny thing was that in the nightmares he still had his own face and the cap hanging over his eye. In a way that was worse than a Morlock's hairy, ape-like face, and when the siren sounded he was stirring the Kia-ora in the Kia-ora machine... and all the kids were queuing up to buy his juice...

For a while the nightmares had bothered him so much that he had stopped going with the gang to the matinee. He could remember those Saturday afternoons without the gang, kicking a puckered ball against the wall of the house, playing at Patience, throwing stones at nothing in particular, torturing the cat... Then one Saturday he'd plucked up the courage to go back to the cinema, although he was still scared of the Morlocks and the darkness that would happen when the lights went down and the golden curtains opened. And it had been all right, the film had made him forget all about the Morlocks — until now.

He looked along the row at all the faces bathed in the bluish light from the screen, staring up at the film. They looked so stupid, so dumb and stupid and hypnotised. They were like the zombies of paradise, their mouths hanging open, their eyes staring up at the screen. When the film finished, when the siren sounded, then they'd have to go and meet the Morlocks who waited for them at home, stirring the cauldrons...

He started laughing silently to himself at the idea of it. Christine felt his chest shaking, turned to look at him and said: "What?"

He shook his head and said: "Nothing."

But Christine could always tell when he was keeping something to himself. She persisted: "What is it? Tell me!"

When he still didn't tell her — it was too long and complicated and anyway she wouldn't find it funny — she pretended to be annoyed. Maybe she was really annoyed, but it looked like she was acting. Acting was something they did together all the time. She acted sad; he acted concerned. Or he acted moody and she acted cheerful. Or she acted annoyed, and he acted like a fool to get her out of it. It wasn't like real acting, the kind they did in films. It was a different kind of acting, because the feelings were real, but it was like the two of them were just trying the feelings on for size, like clothes to see if they fitted, and to see if they suited them.

In a way, he quite liked it when she was annoyed with him. It did suit her. She had dark eyelashes, and when she was being annoyed she looked down, so that all you could see was the eyelashes and the wide mouth turning down at the corners. It made her look mysterious. It was like he was seeing a side of her he didn't know. Also, he felt, it was maybe a side of her she didn't really know either.

Once, he had made her cry. What his pals had been saying to him about her had been getting to him, so he'd decided to chuck her. They'd gone for a walk in the graveyard that night. It had been a lovely sunny evening. Everything had been fine except that at the back of his mind he knew that he was going to have to tell her it was finished. Then they went into a bit of the church that was sort of half outside and half inside. In the cool shadows they'd kissed and canoodled. Then he'd told her. She'd turned away, but he'd seen the long black mascara tears trailing down her cheeks. It looked like her eyes were melting, like she was really "crying her eyes out".

He'd felt so bad about her crying, and missed her so much, that a few days later he'd knocked on the door of the girls' bogs at dinner time and asked for her. When she'd come out, he'd taken her along to the Maths corridor and asked her if she'd have him back. She'd thrown her arms around him and looked happier than he'd ever seen her before, happier than he'd ever seen anyone.

Maybe it wasn't all acting, even if they didn't know how they should do it or say it.

He noticed that she'd stopped chewing her gum and was still looking really annoyed. He asked her: if she'd finished with it, could he borrow it?

It didn't work.

In the end he had to tell her. About the roller skates, the Kia-ora man, the Morlocks in the wardrobe and the zombies of paradise. About the nightmares and being scared of the dark when the lights went down at the matinee. What he couldn't tell her about, what he couldn't find words to explain, was the idea that all the folk around them were just like the zombies of paradise, and when they left the cinema it was like the siren sounding. The Morlocks would be waiting for them... but he couldn't tell her that. She knew it anyway. She knew that if she missed the bus and had to walk home and if she got in late, the Morlocks would be waiting for her, stirring the cauldron...

She listened to it all and when he'd finished whispering it in her ear she moved away from him and said: "Is that all?"

But she kissed him quickly on the cheek, looked at him as if she was looking from far away and smiled. It was just a little kiss, but one of the things he liked about Christine, although everybody said she was a dog, was that she was a great kisser, she had all these different kinds of kisses. All of her kisses made him feel good inside, made him feel like himself, like he was acting in a film but the part he was playing was himself. It was magic, and sometimes when he was with her he wanted to shout something out but he didn't know what.

He put his arms round her and let his fingers play with the gold chain of her locket. She went back to the film, her mouth opening and closing as she chewed her gum.

David Bowie was watching fifty televisions at once, all showing different programmes. He kept changing all the channels with his handset. Christine's hand covered his mouth before he could shout it out: "*Nothin much on telly the night!*"

Anyway, it wasn't very funny. Not worth getting thrown out for.

But Christine was laughing because of what she was doing, putting her hand over his mouth to shut him up. She was still laughing a bit when he moved his hand up to her neck, pulled her closer and kissed her on the mouth. Then the laugh died away in her throat and they started kissing seriously. He could taste her lipstick and her gum, feel the tips of her teeth and her moist, soft tongue... He stroked her neck, then ran his hand down over her shoulder, down over her collarbone... before he could go any further, she caught his hand in hers and squeezed it.

After a while they broke apart and watched the film.

David Bowie was having his nipples removed with a scalpel. Christine hissed: "Don't you dare."

Anyway he couldn't think of anything very funny to shout out, apart from maybe: "*Ohyah!*"

What would it really be like to fall to Earth? Sometimes he wondered about that. Sometimes he could even feel that he really just had fallen to Earth, like when he looked along the row and saw all the faces staring up at the screen. It was like seeing people for the first time. Not one at a time, the way you usually looked at them, but sitting there in a row, like a line of aliens, like the zombies of paradise.

They held each other close in the newsagent's doorway, waiting for the bus. They kissed, but his mind was only half on what he was doing. He wanted to tell her that she wasn't like the others, not a zombie of paradise, and that she suited her nose or it suited her, and that he liked her eyes, her mouth, her hair, the way she laughed... He wanted to tell her something he had never told anybody else.

Why couldn't he say it to her, just look into her eyes and say it? Of course, it wasn't like saying something ordinary, although, going by the films, people said it to each other all the time. He should forget about looking into her eyes when he said it. He should just, after a really long kiss, a serious kiss like this one, whisper it in her ear, and it would sound as loud and as real as the soundtrack of a film. Or just say it, say it like he meant it, say it like he wasn't acting at all. The trouble was he'd never said it to anybody before and he wondered if she might laugh. If she did, he didn't know what he'd do. If she laughed, he'd probably look for a fight on the way home.

"Here it comes."

She snatched another quick kiss and broke away from him and hurried to the door of the bus. She turned to him, smiled and waved as the bus door opened. Then she went on, paid her fare and found a seat next to the window so that she could smile and wave again. It was only when the bus started to pull away from the stop that he panicked inside and he didn't care who heard as he shouted, shouted, shouted it out.

LIZ LOCHHEAD

*I write poems, plays for the stage and, sometimes, for radio and television. And screenplays, which rarely get made in the end, although I wrote a short drama, **Latin For A Dark Room**, which was shot in Edinburgh and Glasgow in the spring of 1994. (The outlet is film festivals and two BBC television screenings.) Most of all I want to write more poems, because they've been getting fewer, and I miss the very special excitement of writing these things, which are for nothing and no one except themselves, setting their own deadlines. I'd also like someday to have enough short stories for a book of them. I live in Glasgow with my husband. No kids, no dog.*

*"The Cure" is a first-person short story — **not** a "dramatic monologue", which — to me — is a play for one person and an audience wherein there is a **conflict** between the story the character of the speaker **thinks** she or he is telling and the story the audience **hears**. All my dramatic monologues, and I have written very many, for performance, are based on this gap. All have — more or less — "unreliable narrators". Gemma in "The Cure" is not like this. In fact I see no reason not to believe she is telling us the absolute truth about her own thoughts and feelings. I don't think Gemma is kidding herself? My pleasure in writing her is to ask myself such questions, and to see if I can somehow, with nothing but a voice create a character and a situation, and make her come alive from the word go. Her voice is (I hope) totally different from my own voice. I made the story up. It amazes me that if you use the "I" it seems you have to explain this to people!*

BOOKS BY LIZ LOCHHEAD

Dreaming Frankenstein and Collected Poems and *True Confessions and New Cliches* (Polygon)
Blood and Ice (Methuen)
Tartuffe (trans. into Scots: Polygon/Third Eye Publications)
Mary Queen of Scots Got Her Head Chopped Off, Dracula and *Bagpipe Muzak* (Penguin)
Three Scottish Poets: MacCaig/Morgan/Lochhead (Cannongate Classics)

The Cure

He goes: Aha, the very one I've been looking for.

I'm like, who me? Feeling this big beamer of a riddy creep up on my face. Trying to do a mind over matter over blushing.

He goes: Gemma, the very girl. Listen, Gems, you're gonny run the Intermediate Inter-House Mixed Relay, right?

I'm like that.

He says: Gie's a brekk, Gemma, don't look at us like that, you're white as a sheet, you'd think I'd asked you to do something scary or something. C'mon I've ticked your name alreadys, ask not what your House can do for you, ask what you can do for your House. Which is a measly hunner yards. Wan leg of a relay. A scoosh. Your Country Needs You.

And he points at us like yon Uncle Sam Poster.

Och, away an —

Yes, Gemma?

Nuh. N.A.W. No way Ho-zay. I'm no daen it. That's what I should of says. All I get out, but, is: I canny ... *please* don't ... don't ask me.

But he got round us. Roy Speedie, House-Captain. Man of my dreams. The only person I've ever fancied.

He got round us. Dead easy. Would not take no for an answer. Pardon. I didn't catch that. You see I need you, Gemma, simple as that. You're running.

'Parently total shortage of females in the third year with initials between the letter S and the end of the alphabet, thus qualifying them as bonafidy born members of Dalhousie House, Staneyburn High. Seems there's just yon Robina Smiley (the fastest runner, swimming champion, centre-forward intermediate first eleven hockey team, Dux of the Year, Captain of the Debating Team, leader of the God Squad, Duke of Edinburgh Award blah, blah,

blah, etcetera) — well, *she's* running obviously. Then there's Julie Ann Taylor, who's just had the twins, Donna Scrimgeour, ME, Elaine Yuill, anorexia, and big gi-normous Sandra Veitch (glandular fat, no puppy). And me. Theory is I'll be best of a bad lot. Just cos I'm dead average-ish. Dead average-ish and dead dead-against sport of any kind.

Except — don't ask me why — late-night snooker on the telly. Mibbe it's because it reminds me of staying up late with my Dad when I was wee and getting a toty wee splash of lager into my lemonade and him going wheest, don't tell your mammy and winking, and then me thinking I was IT, imagining my head was spinning because I'd drank a whole glass of shandy. He still watches the snooker with us when I go over to his during the holidays. We bet five ps. Other times at home I watch it myself because mum can't abide it.

Running, but. I'd run a mile from the very idea. Only Roy Speedie willny let us.

Janine Marshall and Margo Capaldi were smarming all over us the minute he'd left me. So. What did big Speedie want? Did he ask you out? I seen you blushing. Eh? What was he after? You gaun wi him to the Senior Disco? He really *likes* you, Gems. It's dead obvious intit, Margo? Oh aye, did you see the wey he smiled at her, eh, J?

Listen, here's my advice to you, and if you have any sense you'll take it. You fancy somebody, say nothing. Nothing. To nobody.

Look, I know how it is. You fall for somebody and it builds up. Inside. This feeling. An excitement. All the time. Dizzy and that. The usual. Say it's the first time, ever, that it's ever happened to you, you recognise it right away. As in the books, songs, movies. Yup, here you go. This is it. And the next thing, because you can't resist it at the time, you're blurting out to your best pal, just for the pure pleasure of saying his name out loud — which might feel, temporarily, like it's a release and a good idea — the whole true-confession, listen, I-am-daft-about-so-and-so *mistake*. Which it is. Mibbe you can't help your feelings, but surely to god you can zip your mouth?

Wish I hud.

Instead I have to repeat to them what Roy Speedie has said. How it doesn't matter how badly I run in the race, the important thing is to try my best. For the sake of the team. For the sake of the House. That is all anybody can ask of me. That's all I can ask of myself. That's all Roy Speedie is asking.

I still think that's him working up to asking you out, goes Margo.

See what I mean about regretting that I opened my stupit trap? I might have had the pleasure of fantasising that myself. But hearing Margo coming out with it forces me to recognise it for the pathetic delusion it is. Margo doesn't believe it for a minute either. This is just the kind of crap your pals seem to be obliged to come out with. When they know your secret heart's desire.

The week leading up to the sports is a nightmare. I can't sleep. I feel sick. All I can think of is that unless I get run over by a bus or carted off to the hospital in an ambulance with a burst appendix, I will have to appear in front of the whole school in my gym shorts with my bare legs all measled wi granny's tartan with sitting reading too close to the gas fire all winter, and my Mum's aerobics trainers. Me, who am strictly a thick black tights and Doc Marten person. And, in front of the whole school, I will have to run. Despite the fact that, until I learned good foolproof skives to avoid such embarrassments, I regularly came in last in any heat of any first year athletic event. And Helen Paterson laughed at us, called us spiderlegs, and imitated me running by tying her knees together with a gym sash and then splayfooting along with sticky-out elbows waggling out of time till everybody knotted themselves.

My mother has no sympathy. She hopes I think nobody will have anything better to do with their time than look at me. Just do my best and that's all anybody can ask. She's never heard so much girning about nothing.

She's washed and pressed my gym kit.

The day of the sports is brilliant sunshine. It would be. Once the dreaded moment has arrived, but, I am strangely calm. Roy Speedie has already won the Senior 200 metres and the hurdles, and Dalhousie and Balfour Houses are running neck and neck in the Inter-House competition, so he and the Balfour House captains, a scrawny red-haired guy with white eyelashes called Billy Molyneux and a big blowsy girl with the very unfortunate name of Judy Peasgood, are pep-talking their teams for the Intermediate Inter-House Mixed Relay. Us. Balfour have just won the Junior Inter-House Relay and Dalhousie a very close second. Roy smiles at us. It's a great smile and I am not, myself, impressed by Janine Marshall's past comment that he doesny half know it. He smiles. Right at me. Similar melting effect as the day six months ago when I fell madly in love with him during Paul Jones at third year Christmas Dance. Senior House captains and prefects were also invited, although very few of the *female* prefects, funnily enough, bothered to turn up. Sixth year *guys* did, but. An obvious sickner for the acned beanpoles or waver-voiced smouts or specky swots with charisma bypasses that make up the boys in our year. So, when the music stopped, and there's Roy Speedie exactly half way between me and Judy Peasgood in a figured velvet frock that made her look like a settee or something, he just shrugs, smiles at me, takes my hands and whirls me away into the Gay Gordons, during which he asks my name — my name! — and holds me dead tight in the polka-ing bit so's he can get an extra birl in. When the music changes he winks at us, that smile again, and he's off. And I am in love. I recognised it right away. I keep it up for months. Nothing changes. Nothing particular seems to need to happen to keep it going. An occasional sighting, a walk past his house with Janine Marshall and an argument over whether that was him or his dad sitting there in front of the blue flickery light of the TV. Him walking past in the dinner school. This will do, apparently.

And now the race. I have to do my best, that's all. Like I says, it's weird but I'm — suddenly — dead calm. An absence of butterflies. I walk to the third place. I'm on third. The team goes: Ronnie Urquhart, Robina Smiley, me, then Alasdair Speedie, Roy's wee brother.

Nobody could fancy *him*. Ever.

The race itself is weird. Time jerks from slow motion to speeded up then back again. On your marks, dead slow, get set, slower still, and *go*. Ronnie Urquhart is barrelling along with his head down and his arms going like pistons, but it's as if he's standing still, then, suddenly, he's round the bend and I've just got time to realise he's in the lead and the changeover to Robina Smiley is already made, clockwork, and she's charging towards me full tilt with a purple face and the mouth in it opens, Run! Run!, and she looks daggers, raging, honest if looks could kill, and my wee legs have finally started up but I'm still gawping at her and she's skelped the baton home into my mitt and the other third-person runners are starting up, one, two and three and they're after me getting the baton, God, Dalhousie must be in the lead, but, by the time I realise that, they're past me, and I'm doing my best, doing my best, giving it laldy, shoes skliffing off the gravel, it speeds up again, and jigging in front of me is the furious face of Roy's wee brother, c'mon, *c'mon*. and he's the last of the fourths still on his mark, he starts running, too quick, too quick, I can't catch him, he slows down again, slows down practically till a standstill, slows down slow enough till I can complete the baton pass, even then I nearly drop it, but, eventually, away he goes like the clappers into all the shouting and I'm finally doubled up, peching, with a stitch in my side as they cross the line, Balfour, Aitken, Crimmond and, last but not least, a poor fourth, Dalhousie. Bringing up the cow's tail.

Next thing Roy Speedie is by my side and he's screaming at me. You stupit, stupit bitch. We were winning, we were *first* and *you* — I stand back up straight. My stitch is gone. I seem to have my puff back. I feel ... fantastic. This time it's me that smiles at him. I even consider winking. I shrug, but. I says: I tried my best. As you said yourself, nobody can ask more than that, Roy. And away I go to get changed.

Janine Marshall and Margo Capaldi seem to have difficulty believing it, but I am completely cured of love for Roy Speedie. They give me pitying glances when Roy Speedie and Robina Smiley — they seem to have taken up with each other — moon past hand in hand up the park at lunch time. They think I'm being brave when I say I'm not bothered. Margo says they deserve each other, Smiley Speedie and Speedy Smiley, but, quite honestly, it is a matter of no interest to me. As I fell in love with him in an instant, so I fell out of love with him in an instant and now I am immune to his pointless good looks.

As, at the same time, I grew out of the Glory of The School, Do Your Best, Healthy Competition, Pillar of the British Empire, Second Hand Imitation Public School carry-on. I mean, you look at Staneyburn, the pit shut, empty acres of industrial estate, the high street with half the shops boarded up (bar Poundstretcher) twenty folk trying to sell you the *Big Issue* to wan flogging *Militant*; and our school, which, despite its golden past as a Senior Secondary, is just a local comprehensive pure and simple, tries to uphold the idea that the most important thing is winning the House Shield and being elected by a jury of your peers to high office and the wearing of the Prefects' Braid. And is there honey still for tea? Get real.

I became, the instant I fell out of love with Roy Speedie, one of the apathetic ones the headmaster castigates in school assembly. This thought makes me quite cheery. Inside myself I have a laboratory of interesting emotions. I am a woman of experience. I have fallen in love. I have fallen out of love. Someday, mibbe when they grow up a bit, Janine Marshall and Margo Capaldi might understand.

ALISON FELL

I was born in Dumfries but later moved to Hamilton, then the Highlands, and then back to a village near Lockerbie. I now live in London. Apart from school English compositions, I started writing my own stories when I was about 12. These were wild sagas of girls with long glamorous hair and cleavages captured at knife-point by Mexican bandits, etc! I did illustrations for them, and circulated them among my friends, thus gaining quite a bit of status. Later, at 16, I started to write poetry (not rhyming — I hated the eighteenth- and nineteenth-century poets we studied in English Literature) and published one in (I think) **Scotland Magazine** *while I was still at Dumfries Academy. The poetry I wrote was the only thing that seemed to satisfy my inner moods, since at that time I was hopeless at understanding my feelings or talking about them in any direct way. In adult life I've gone on to write novels rather more than poetry (you can't make a living as a poet in this Philistine country) but poetry remains for me the centre, the life-blood.*

In January 1994 I saw a small but shocking TV news item about an oil town in Siberia where the workers hadn't been paid for months. The Co-Operative stores, which gave credit, had run out of supplies, and people were beginning to starve — in the 1990s, in a developed industrial country! So this is what started me off on the story. My other theme was the awful longing to be **thin** *that many girls have nowadays, when anorexic fashion models like Kate Moss are the standard of beauty. For the first time in history, starvation has actually become* **fashionable** *…*

Since I've never been to Siberia (but have always wanted to go on the Trans Siberian Railway) I had to do a little research — looking at atlases to work out a suitable but fictitious name for the town, checking a few details about the changeover from communism to capitalism, etc. Usually I do a lot of research — for my last novel, which is set in tenth-century Japan, I spent weeks reading in the British Museum Library — but this story came far more from my own childhood images of the Highlands, of snowdrifts and deer hunts and frozen rivers. And for me that's usually how a poem or story begins — it's a kind of chase. An image nags at me, and I have to follow it, until I see why it fascinates me and where it leads. I hardly ever know what the plot will be, *or how the story will end. If I did, I'd probably get bored and give up — there wouldn't be enough excitement in it. Writing is about exploration, really, about **not knowing** where you're going, but having to take the trip all the same, for the pleasure and risk of it!*

BOOKS BY ALISON FELL

Novels
The Grey Dancer (Collins Fontana)
Every Move You Make (Virago)
The Bad Box (Methuen)
The Crystal Owl (Methuen)
Mer de Glace (Serpent's Tail)
The Pillow Boy of the Lady Onogoro (Serpent's Tail)

Poetry
Kisses for Mayakovsky (Virago)
The Crystal Owl (Virago)

Our Lady of the Mammoths

"This young lady, now, was carved out of ivory from a mammoth's tusk," said the museum curator, beaming over the glass case at the High School students. "Not only did she reign over the mysteries of childbirth, but our cave-dwelling ancestors also prayed to her for luck in the hunt."

Valeria Semyonova frowned severely at the statue in the case, so that Alexei Timov — Sasha to his friends — wouldn't winkle out her embarrassment. The naked female had a tadpole head, ribbon arms, and consisted almost entirely of buttocks, fat belly, and huge swollen breasts. Lower down, the pubic triangle stared shamelessly back at her. The curator, who had bristly orange hair and braces, and looked hardly older than the school students, rattled on in his high nervous voice.

"She really is a fine example of the Great Mother Goddess of the Aurignacian period." The young curator smiled hopefully. "Not such a young lady after all, then, is she!" But the joke was too weak, and the students rolled their eyes in contempt.

Miss Andreyevna — not Comrade Andreyevna any more, now that communism had been dumped in the dustbin of history, or so Valeria's father said — came to the curator's rescue. "Now then, can anyone tell us just how old this carving is?" she demanded, in a voice that brooked no nonsense.

"Thirty thousand years," said Sasha instantly, and winked at Valeria, who had seen him read the small typed card on the wooden base of the stand. "Paleo-whatsit, isn't she?"

"Paleolithic," cried the curator in relief. "Well done!"

"Talk about a spare tyre!" said Maria Antonina, the class loudmouth, and everyone, as usual, laughed.

"We wouldn't put her on a magazine cover nowadays," the curator agreed with a smile, "but to our ancestors she was more glamorous than Madonna. She was the one who put the food in the pot, as it were, and kept them all from starving. So to Cro-Magnon man she summed up all the magical force and wonder of the female."

The curator's eyes were bright blue behind pebble glasses. He caught Valeria's curious glance and, before she could look away, smiled shyly. "Here at the museum we call her Our Lady of the Mammoths. We think she's very beautiful."

A titter spread through the group, and Valeria blushed and huddled into the folds of her parka, trying to shrink her unwanted curves to a thin string. She's going to be a big girl, people would say to her grandmother, when all Valeria wanted was to be lean and neat and boyish, like she used to be. She stared angrily out of the window, wondering how anything as fat as the statue could ever be called beautiful. Outside, the larch branches were white nets of snow, and beyond them pinpoints of flame flickered from the tall discharge pipes on the oilfields across the river.

Winter sets in early on the Siberian plateau, and the snow was a white steppe which stretched unbroken from the Tarensk oilfield to the distant mountains. The river Lena, which enclosed the town of Tarensk in a slow horseshoe bend, had been frozen over since early October. It was around then, in the first snap of winter, while the children of Tarensk tested the forbidden ice with their skates, that the trouble had begun.

At first no one had taken it seriously, except perhaps the older people, but then old folks were always pessimists, as far as Valeria could see. What had happened was that on pay day at the oilfields, the workers had queued up as usual, only to be told by a clerk with a very red face that the money had not yet arrived. Some hitch, it seemed, with the Central Bank — but if they would all be patient, their wages would of course be paid out in the course of the next few days. However, week had followed week, and still no wage packets appeared.

"'Economic Reforms'," scoffed Valeria's grandmother, who had no faith in the new capitalism sweeping Russia. "At least under communism the workers got looked after!"

Valeria's father, who worked in the oil refinery, stuck up stoutly for Yeltsin. After all, it was only a minor delay, and since all Tarensk's oil workers were guaranteed credit at the Co-Operative stores, they were hardly in danger of starving to death, were they?

Valeria's grandmother eyed him from the depths of her black shawls. "What do they care what happens out in the sticks?" she sniffed. "They'll throw us all to the wolves, you'll see."

Miss Andreyevna clapped her hands briskly and the tittering stopped. "Now if you'll thank Mr Antipov for his interesting talk, everyone, and I'll expect your history essays on Monday morning."

"Some of us are going skating," said Sasha, catching up with Valeria outside the museum. "Are you coming?"

"I can't," said Valeria curtly, "I've got things to do." She didn't feel like going into detail. If she had to stand yet again in the endless queue at the Co-Op, what business was it of Sasha's?

Sasha flushed and turned on his heel. "Oh, fine. Don't let me keep you from your *chores!*"

Fuming at the unfairness of this, Valeria trudged through the snowy streets to join the queue. Sasha's mother had a job in the Telegraph Office at the station, and could shop anywhere, and pay real money, whereas Valeria could only choose from the dwindling goods in the Co-Operative, and pay with credit coupons.

Since most people in Tarensk were either oil workers or their families, the queue was long, and moved slowly, and when at last Valeria reached the door she could already see how little was left on the shelves. There was no bacon or butter, or sugar or oatmeal, and she arrived at the cash desk with a basket which contained only a tired-looking cabbage, two tins of tomatoes, and half a brown loaf.

"The supplies aren't coming through," said the cashier apologetically. "We don't know what's going on either."

Supper that evening was a meagre affair, despite the efforts of Valeria's grandmother, who could generally conjure a tasty meal from the least promising materials. The news from the oil plant had not improved, and Valeria's father, too weary to take off his overalls, sat silent and grim-faced at the table. To cheer him, Valeria told him about the history lesson, and the strange Stone Age carving in the museum. Her father broke a cigarette in half and lit it, coughing.

"Stone Age, is it? Well, we'll all be back there soon enough if you ask me, shooting crows and grubbing for acorns."

"Oh, come on, Dad," Valeria encouraged, smiling. "I bet the wages turn up tomorrow! It's 1994, remember ..."

That night Valeria dreamt that she was naked and bulbous, like
the ivory goddess. Only she was not in a glass case, and the museum was not a museum but a dimly-lit cave. The flicker of torches
danced on her swollen belly, and on the faces of the people who
stretched their pitifully bony arms towards her, as if begging to be
fed.

Valeria woke from this nightmare with relief. It was Saturday
morning, and she was struggling with her history essay when Sasha
banged on the window. She peered through the icicles, and saw
the dead rabbit dangling from his gloved hand.

"Well, well," said her grandmother, opening the door to him, "if
it isn't Masha Timova's boy!"

"One of the signalmen gave it to my mother," Sasha mumbled
awkwardly. "She's allergic to rabbit, though." The lie was plain as
day, but Valeria bit back her sharp retort, for her grandmother had
already seized the animal and was examining it appreciatively.

"She always was a good comrade, your mother," the old lady
said warmly. From now on, Valeria realised, she would have to
swallow her pride and accept whatever charity was offered, if only
for the sake of her family.

"Come out for a bit?" said Sasha with a shamefaced look. "I'm
on my skis."

To pay him back for yesterday, Valeria was about to refuse, but
her grandmother would have none of it. "Go and get some fresh
air," she insisted. "You'll grow roots if you sit at that table much
longer."

Outside the day was bitterly cold, but clear and blue. Valeria
fetched her old skis from the shed and, turning her back on Sasha,
bent to adjust the bindings. "Listen," said Sasha, "I'm sorry about
yesterday, okay?"

Straightening up, Valeria looked him in the eye. "You can be
really horrible when you feel like it," she said flatly. Then she
gripped her ski-sticks, and pushed, and sped off along the snowy
track which bordered the deer farm. When Sasha caught up with
her his face was red from exertion. He blocked her way with a ski-
stick, frowning sulkily.

"That museum bloke — he was giving you the eye."

"He never was!" Valeria laughed incredulously. "You're not trying to tell me you were jealous!"

Sasha flushed and skidded his skis back and forward, making
slushy ruts in the snow. He muttered something that was drowned
out by the engine of an approaching helicopter. Valeria glanced up
and saw the reindeer hanging upside down from the underbelly.
Their legs had been lashed together and their antlered heads flow-
ered out in a sad, swaying bouquet. They would be stored at the
railway station before being shipped to Moscow or even Japan, for
venison was a prime export these days, or so her father had told
her.

"I said," Sasha repeated doggedly, "I thought he was right —
about the statue being beautiful."

Valeria's heart raced uncomfortably. She felt bulky and self-conscious, and wished he would stop looking at her like that. Her
mind filled with childish retorts: Keep your eyes to yourself, she
wanted to snap.

"That fat old thing!" she scoffed, to hide her confusion, and she
spurred herself on, slipping easily over the frozen crust of the snow.

A second helicopter rose above the trees which surrounded the
deer farm and thundered overhead with its grisly load of reindeer.
Valeria glared up at it, impatiently wiping away a drip of something
wet which fell on to her forehead. Her hand came away red, and
she let out a cry of disgust. Simultaneously she saw the trail of
blood in the snow.

"Oh, *gross!*" said Sasha, catching up with her. He waved a
vicious two-finger sign at the pilot, but the helicopter was already
half a mile away.

On the way back Valeria was tense and silent. Hunger made her
light-headed, and the words of her history book echoed in her
mind like a crazy refrain. *In the Stone Age men ate their meat raw.* She
stopped, panting, on the brow of the hill. Down in the valley she
could see the black scar of the railway track, with the oil pipeline
running alongside it. She turned to Sasha, suddenly frightened.
"They wouldn't really let us starve, Sasha, would they?"

The rabbit stew would have fed Valeria's family for longer if
there had been dumplings to go with it, but there was only half a

cup of flour in the cupboard, and none at all in the shops. The rabbit pelt, meanwhile, hung curing from a hook on the veranda. "It'll make a nice warm hat for that Sasha of yours," said her grandmother, as Valeria set off for school.

"He isn't *mine*," said Valeria, flushing, and banged the door behind her.

At lunch break Sasha came up to her with a serious face. "The train hasn't run since last week," he said. "They're saying it's snow on the track but mum thinks there's something fishy, because the Moscow telephone line's cut out as well."

That night Valeria watched the television news with Sasha and his mother. Maria Timova had some eggs from the signalman admirer, and insisted that Valeria share the thick potato omelette. When the news had ended and the last scrap of omelette had been eaten, they looked at one another in dismay. There had not been the slightest mention of any crisis in a small Siberian oil town called Tarensk. Perhaps Valeria's grandmother had been right from the beginning, and the government in Moscow had abandoned them. It was as if they had simply been wiped off the map.

At the end of the week the Co-Operative shut its doors for the last time. People stood on the icy steps, shaking their heads, appalled. "They've no right!" they cried. "Something's got to be done!" But who could they shout at and who could they blame? The Town Soviet had been disbanded a year ago, and the Town Council, which was intended to take its place, had not yet been elected. Nobody, absolutely nobody, was in charge.

Day after day Valeria's father went off to work, hoping against hope that the wage shipment had arrived. Not that money itself would have solved anything, however, for by this time even the independent shops had run out of supplies, and one by one they shuttered their windows and barricaded their doors and left their despairing customers to fend for themselves as best they could.

With coal supplies running dangerously low, the school went on half time, and Valeria and Sasha spent their afternoons in the countryside, foraging for food. Occasionally they found a smallholding which had a few eggs to sell, and once they came upon a deserted collective farm where cliffs of frosty turnips had been left to rot.

That day they skied home with full knapsacks, but more often than not they returned exhausted and empty-handed.

Hunger was a habit now, and those who were old or feeble suffered most. Valeria's grandmother could no longer keep house, and scarcely had the strength to keep the log fire stoked up. Valeria suspected that she starved herself when left alone in the daytime, to make the food go further.

"Don't waste it on me," she said proudly one evening, as Valeria tried to spoon thin potato soup into her mouth. "I've had my innings. It's yourselves you should be thinking about now."

Valeria's father thumped his fist on the table and uncharacteristically laid down the law. "Stop that nonsense, Mother!" he barked. "It's share and share alike in this house, and don't you forget it!"

A smile flickered weakly across the old woman's face. "So you're a good communist after all, are you, Valery?" she jibed.

In her bedroom mirror Valeria was now as skinny as she could ever have wished; skinnier, in fact, than any fashion model. Her cheekbones stuck out like a Tartar's, and her ribs were as corrugated as a tin roof. She looked at her hollow hipbones and, shivering — for these days she was always cold — she burrowed quickly under her bedcovers.

That night she dreamt she was wrapped in a mammoth skin, the warm fur swaddling her luxuriously. In the dream she called out for Sasha, and he came towards her in his rabbit-fur hat. In his hands was the little fat statue of the goddess, and he cradled her tenderly, and fed her with morsels of bread soaked in milk.

Valeria woke with a start, for it was as if a clear, impatient voice had spoken, like a schoolteacher reminding a pupil of some elementary lesson. *When the people make offerings of food to the goddess, she rewards them one hundredfold with her bounty.* Frightened, she peered into the shadows, but there was no one in the room, only the pale moon staring frostily in at her.

Next day at school Valeria could not bring herself to tell Sasha about the eerie voice, for she was afraid he would laugh at her and call her crazy. She hugged her empty stomach and stared broodingly around the class. How old her friends looked, these days, the girls hollow-cheeked, and the boys' gaunt faces shadowed with bristle, for there were no longer any razor blades to be had. How grown-up hunger makes us, she thought sadly. Even Sasha has lost his mischief. She saw that they were all care-worn, weighed down by their new responsibilities. For they were the young ones, the strong ones, and their families relied on them.

That night when she and Sasha returned from their foraging, Maria Timova hugged them excitedly. Her dark eyes sparkled in her pale exhausted face. "I got through to Sergei at last," she said. "I can't tell you how long it took!" Sergei was a journalist Maria Timova had known since her college days, and who now worked for the BBC World Service. Since Sergei had heard nothing of the suffering in Tarensk, it seemed certain that the news blackout was total. Shocked by the conditions Maria Timova described, he promised to do everything he could to alert his friends in the media. "He says he'll get on to the United Nations if he has to," Maria Timova finished triumphantly.

Eager to share the news, Valeria rushed home and repeated the conversation to her father and grandmother. Her father looked at her bitterly. "Humanitarian aid, is it? So we're a Third World country now, are we?" He turned away from her, and held his hands out to the dwindling fire.

Tears rose to Valeria's eyes, and she looked pleadingly at her grandmother. Was there nothing she could do to please him?

"Don't mind your father," the old lady said in a low voice. "It's because the plant shut down today. They're all laid off."

Next day no one in Tarensk spoke of the silence, but everyone was aware of it. The derricks on the oilfields no longer thudded and clanked, and the pumping station at the head of the pipeline no longer hummed day and night. Only the tall discharge pipes in the distance continued to send out their useless pinpoints of flame, like candles on some forgotten altar.

Valeria had not meant to stop at the museum, for she was already late for class, but somehow her skis would go no further than St Basil's Square, where she found herself standing in front of the shabby wooden building which huddled like a poor relation in the shadow of the big modern church.

Inside she made her way through the dusty galleries until she came to the room where the goddess stood proud and alone in her glass case. Valeria glanced around and, judging that the coast was clear, she stopped furtively and placed a small piece of pickled cucumber on the wooden frame of the case.

A sudden noise behind her made her spin round guiltily. Antipov the curator stood in the doorway, coughing harshly. He looked very thin, and his new dark beard was a bad match for his dyed orange hair.

"Don't worry," he muttered, holding on to the door frame for support. "You're not the only one who's making offerings. Our Lady of the Mammoths gets more queues than the Co-Op these days." He laughed weakly, and another spasm of coughing shook his body. "She hasn't had so much attention for millenia!" And then Antipov ran a hand over his eyes, staggered, and fainted on the floor at Valeria's feet.

It was Sasha who helped her drag the sledge to the hospital, and waited with her while the doctor made his rapid diagnosis. "Pneumonia due to malnutrition," he said. "Our wards are over-flowing with it."

"Will he be all right?" asked Valeria, staring as if hypnotised at the bluish-grey face of the curator.

"I'm sorry," said the doctor, with a curt shake of his head, as he pulled the white sheet over the incongruous orange hair.

Valeria wept into Sasha's shoulder as they stood by the empty sleigh. She thought of her father and grandmother, she thought of Sasha's mother, so pale and gaunt, yet who still wore a brave splash of red lipstick every day, and refused to give in to despair.

If we're to die, she thought, with a sudden feeling of calm, I want us all to be together.

Sasha was silent, and held her tightly, as if he had sensed her thoughts. After a long time he said, "Valya, why don't we go up on the hill. You can see such a long way from there."

On the brow of the hill Valeria lay down in the snow and stared blankly at the sky. It was blue as glass and not a bird moved in it. Sasha knelt down beside her and rubbed her cold hands roughly, trying to warm them. "Don't give in, Valya," he pleaded. "We're not finished yet!"

Valeria closed her eyes, and for a blissful moment the snow enfolded her as generously as the mammoth skin in her dream. Silence spread up from the town and stole into the core of her. How peaceful it is, she thought wonderingly. She could not understand why Sasha was shaking her so, or what he was pointing at. Dimly she heard the drone of a helicopter, and saw the corpse of a deer detach itself from the dreadful bouquet, and fall slowly, spiralling, as if in a dream.

"Get up, Valya!" Sasha ordered. "I'm going for the sledge. Can't you see it? Down there in the gully. Go and cover it up in case they come back for it."

Valeria forced herself down the hill and scooped snow over the still-warm body, but the helicopter did not return. When they had loaded the dead deer on the sledge, they looked at each other in terrible uncertainty. What were they to do with the carcass? They could hide it in Valeria's cellar, certainly, save it for their own families and live off it all winter. But how could they hoard their bounty when all around them died of hunger?

It was Sasha who spoke first. "Well we can't keep it for ourselves, can we?" he said gruffly.

Valeria nodded slowly. She knew as well as he did how many mouths there were to feed, and what the decision meant. Fairly divided, the carcass would feed the townsfolk for a day, but no longer. "Share and share alike," she said.

"Right," said Sasha, "We'll take it to the Square, then."

Dusk had fallen by the time they reached the town. Valeria's father and Maria Timova had hurried ahead to spread the word, and when the sledge with its precious burden entered the Square the townsfolk were waiting, silent and fur-clad, their faces lit by flickering hemp torches.

A small table had been set up on the steps of the museum, and on it stood the naked statue of Our Lady of the Mammoths. It was, Valeria realised, almost as she had seen it in her dream — the torches, the gaunt and starving tribes, the goddess with her huge and bountiful breasts. She thought of poor Antipov the curator, who had always worshipped her, and tears filled her eyes. Brushing them away, she motioned to Grishkov the butcher, who stepped forward with his long knives. Deftly he quartered the carcass, and carved the quarters into smaller joints, until everything was divided equally, even the liver and the lights.

One by one the townspeople filed up the steps with their bowls and carrier bags, and collected their share. And the men shook Sasha by the hand, and the women kissed Valeria on the cheek, wiping the tears from their eyes. One old lady, quite overcome, curtseyed to Valeria and said, in an awe-struck whisper, "Bless you, My Lady."

Most people accepted their ration with quiet dignity, but Yuri Kuragin the plumber took his portion with trembling hands and, maddened by hunger, tore at the raw meat with his teeth until blood ran down his chin and froze in scarlet drops in the snow at his feet. "Enough of that, friend!" growled an old man, restraining him kindly enough. "We're civilised here, remember."

At last it was done, and the Square was empty, and the smell of roasting venison spread through the streets of the town. At least for this one night, nobody would starve, and could banish from mind, with an effort of will, all their thin tomorrows.

That night not only Sasha and Valeria, but all the citizens of Tarensk went to bed with full stomachs, and slept a sleep undisturbed, for once, by the cries of hungry infants — a sleep so sound, as it happened, that few were awake to greet the heavy-bellied plane with the UN markings which landed at first light on the solid midwinter ice of the Lena river.

A.L. KENNEDY

I was born in 1965 in Dundee and went to school there until I was seventeen when I left for Warwick University. I always had an interest in theatre, so I took a degree in Theatre Studies and Drama. Around that time I wrote pieces of drama.

Once I graduated, I found it difficult to get a job. Writing is actually the only thing I can do. Although I had been making up stories since I was able to think, this didn't occur to me as a possible job.

I have now had two collections of short stories published and two novels. I have also written a play and I am now working on another novel.

I am very lucky — I love writing and I now earn my living by doing just that. I have even been given awards for writing I did simply because I enjoyed it. I didn't plan things this way, but I certainly have no complaints.

"The Park" arrived after a talk with an English class at Bathgate Academy who reminded me of a park I once went to.

The story-teller or narrator says "you" instead of "I", which is unusual. This way of writing has difficulties — I hope it's intimate and direct, but it could also just seem bossy. "You" could catch the readers' attention, or it could annoy them. Readers will have their own opinion on how well it works for them and each one will be right.

This is a story about growing up, finding new emotions, loss of innocence and the beginnings of guilt — some things I remember about being around 13 or 14. Emotions are usually hard to write about clearly, but I've tried my best to suggest them through mood and a natural flow of information. I don't like to give lectures. Or read them.

The story's subjects are serious, but the narrator is standing back from his or her problems by making jokes. (I sometimes do the same thing). Hopefully humour also makes the story easier to swallow.

You don't know the sex of the narrator — does this help you feel close to him or her?

This story is about some of the things that can go wrong with life and some of the choices the story-teller might be making. I hope he or she mainly makes the right ones and grows up happy.

BOOKS BY A.L. KENNEDY

Night Geometry and the Garscadden Trains (Polygon)
Looking for the Possible Dance (Secker and Warburg)
Now That You're Back (Jonathan Cape)
So I Am Glad (Jonathan Cape)

The Park

You are going to the park now because everyone took you to church today and it was no good. Really.

They packed you into the back seat of Uncle Henry's dying car and there you had to stay. You came from where you live to the edge of the city with your shoulders crushed in by other shoulders and with half of your face being grated into a wiry overcoat — a button just over your eye, you could have been blinded — and with your hips mashed down at a totally unpleasant angle and everything jigging and squeezing and rolling along with the movements of the road.

Nobody asked if you would like this. As it happened, you didn't like this and, as it happened, nobody asked.

You'd been nagged at for years to walk and stand and sit with your shoulders straight up and down and not to slouch about like a mobile apology. You had also been told that you should never snuggle legs and sides together in the rear seats of vehicles, moving or not. But there you were being slowly pressed and folded out of any likely shape and nobody turned a hair.

Never know the minute, do you?

You spent, in fact, thirty-four minutes rasping up against your grandfather at one side — nothing but vicious joints and agony on fast corners — and your Uncle Henry — very like a sandbag — at the other. You were alone with most of your family, glued inside a rotting Lada on a slow, wet autumn day.

This was all no good because you do not have a naturally close family. None of you really likes getting too near. To stand within shouting distance will often be more than enough, which meant that everyone with you on your journey was wishing themselves invisible, faces wild with embarrassment. No one was looking and no one was speaking and no one was doing anything other than closing their eyes and making believe they were not there.

Condensation oozed down the windows while your fellow passengers attempted to inhale in whatever spaces they could find. Breathing out was a completely bad idea. Uncle Henry, who has no sense of rhythm, sucked and blew in limping waltz time and made an odd bubbling noise in his chest. You wished you could open a window.

Your mother parked steadily to a halt through a storm of advice and with Grandfather swinging gleefully out at one door to shout at the pavement and then fend if off with his stick. You waited while he and Uncle Henry exploded on to the kerb, ruffling and straightening and finally walking apart as if they had never been related or even introduced.

And you moved on into the church.

Family decision — today we will be religious and so will you.

You stood in its doorway and you smelled its dry, high, echoing insides. Church. There's no way to like it. No way that you know. It is the only building you can look at and be sure it's looking back.

Not that you didn't once go to church every Sunday morning, winning an attendance prize not very long before you and both your parents stopped attending. And not that you didn't find yourself quite comfy inside churches, because children can feel comfy almost anywhere. And not that you're now possessed by demons or about to come out in a blasphemous rash as soon you're dragged across the threshold. Not at all, nothing so dramatic.

You are just different now. When you step inside the church now you are not a child. You know that and you know the church does, too. The sound of your feet and the tiny cough you make to clear your throat rockets up and off the bare tiling and the hard plaster walls. You want to sneak. Every move or thought of moving bounces from floor to ceiling and back again among the rows and rows of bare, dark pews and, if careless noise is so clear here, you can start to believe your ideas may also be out there on display. What you are and what you do and what you have done are ringing out like fire alarms. Alarms from the big, bad fire.

Now if God is really anywhere, He is here and watching very hard because this is His house, after all, and so you find yourself listing your slyness, your hiding and your sliding and your lots of little lies.

You would like to say, "I've never done anyone any harm. My life's only working things out — it's hardly started yet. I haven't even finished school and nothing is serious so far. Not seriously serious. I mean, it's a bit of fun, really — this life business. You know? I mean, don't you have a sense of humour?"

Then you remember. You really remember. You do things you are fond of — maybe bad things, but not *that* bad, for goodness sake — and you don't want to give them up. You don't care if they're good or not good, you want them with you. Perhaps this could be serious, could mean something serious, you're not sure. You need to think, so you go to the park.

The park is two different places.

It is the park where you went on some weekends with your mother or your father or your mother *and* your father, the two of them there with each other at the same time, because they often liked each other then. You only came to visit in good weather, so this park is daylit and sunshiny and on holiday. Here pitch and putt can be pitched and putted and somebody older than you will always pay. Friendly dogs jump and flop with each other in a non-sexual manner while happy children show their happiness on swings and slides and see-saws and roundabouts, which should really begin with an "s" because everything else does.

On a very few mornings this is also the park of mad, deep snow in genuine drifts that will swallow legs and wellingtons whole without a sound. This is a park suddenly bleached foreign and full of young brains sledging and sliding fearlessly down hillsides and between rhododendrons. Or into rhododendrons. Warnings against snowballs with hidden ice and gravel, lurking pneumonia and nasty boys made every park winter magnificent and also brought them closer to the other park, the one you visit now.

Up above the eternally emptied paddling pool and the water-logged putting green, real life begins. Here you follow the smallest paths and find corners, the longer grass and benches, the places where you need not be seen. There are gardener's bothies, compost dumps, thickets where you will be safe because here you are a freedom fighter, you are wildlife, you are whatever you want to be as long as you can be it privately.

Keep walking and you'll reach the graveyard — rows of hideaways between last century's comfortable dead. Tidy signs warn of falling headstones, vandalised by gravity and time and vandals. The stones themselves have their own stiff or sentimental sentences with, chiselled across them all, "Pray for the repose of the soul of ... Pray for the repose of the soul of ... Pray for the repose of the soul of ..." asking that one peculiar favour of strangers. Behind the soberly recorded families, you can find the bottles, lovingly drained; the carefully abandoned cans — cider and lager and aerosol and glue — with the dirty crisp bags and the strange remains of more peculiar favours.

During the war they took away the railings of this park to make bombs and now it lies open in the night with nothing to defend it but a little list of rules. You have already found the circle of dead trees — meant to have been struck by lightning when God got annoyed — which marks out the meeting place of your local Hell's Angel chapter. You have thought about them. You have listened to their motorbikes. You have come to this park by yourself and you have come here with other people and quite possibly broken its rules, certainly talked about all the rules which should be broken. Breaking rules is very like being free.

Which is very like leaving the house and running here to the park and continuing to run along narrower and narrower tarmacs, over grass, across mud, between tree trunks and bushes and ivy-covered graves without seeing or feeling one thing because you are racing your head. You are trying to out-run your thoughts. You are pushing for that moment when you can fall down on to the ground and lie still with your throat aching and the air raw in your chest and your ears stuffed full of nothing but your pulse and not an idea in your skull. Not a word. You have run everything away and into peace. You are like a small bit of peace.

You would guess they were kneeling to look for some peace in that church. Bowed heads in an almost deserted building; your grandfather and grandmother and Uncle Henry, three overcoated monkeys in a line. Hear nothing, see nothing, say nothing and be a nice family. Give us peace.

You sat a few rows behind and were surprised when your mother slipped up beside you and put her fingers over yours. With her other hand shielding her eyes from nothing anyone could see, she tugged you down to kneel beside her on the little upholstered thing provided for kneeling down on.

You couldn't tell what she was thinking, saying, praying. Her lips did not move, but eventually one or two tears began to drip slowly off her chin. Tears always seem thicker than water. You closed your eyes and avoided seeing how young and small your mother looks when she cries. You've never liked it when she cries.

It seemed natural that you should shelter your eyelids under your free hand, and the darkness this made was comforting and private. You thought that if you chose to pray, this would probably be how you'd do it because there was something right about the way it felt.

You knelt with your mother, eyes covered, both praying or not praying, a tiny family tradition being passed along. You wondered what your father was doing at home. He must have known what was going on, that people were praying about him. Did he feel he should send up a word in his defence?

Probably he was already up higher than you or the church. That was how he lived his life now. Up. On any excuse, he would walk out and up. Maybe there would have been flying pots and door-slams, maybe he would be drunk and maybe he would not, it wouldn't matter. In his face you could see that it couldn't matter because he was going up — up and on to the roof.

He would hint at broken gutters and loose tiles, work he should do, but he never went up there with tools, not even a hammer. He would only sit. You could see him from the street, the man who sat up on his roof even when it was raining. Or inside you could stand under the stairwell and his shadow would be there across the skylight, short and still. You sometimes feel sorry for him.

Last week he went up after three entirely silent days and for the first time you noticed the tremor in his hands as he pulled the attic ladder down and you wondered if he might be afraid of heights. Was he stoking up his vertigo or trying to drive it away? You didn't like to ask him.

You made a ham sandwich for your lunch because it was Saturday and you were at home. You ate standing up in the kitchen, exactly as if you were waiting for your mother to scream.

Your mother screamed.

Running towards the sound you found her looking up at another noise, an uneven rhythm of feet, a sliding thud. Your father's shadow was jumping across the glass sky light. The brightness of his yellow pullover shone through the grubby glass as he crossed over and over. Taking little rests now and then, he jumped all day and into the night.

You could see that your mother was thinking of turning off the hallway lamp which was shining up and letting him keep on jumping, even in the dark. You watched her trying to work out if a lack of light would make him stop and come in, or just keep on risking it. If he made a mistake, he would spring through and down the stairwell for thirty feet.

Finally, your mother went and called on your right-hand neighbours, who were also watching your father jump, because people get fascinated with very odd things sometimes. Your mother likes your right-hand neighbours better than the left while you disagree, because the left-hand neighbours are more happy, even though they're much less reliable in an emergency. The family needs neighbours who are good in an emergency.

You wait in the stairwell, now wondering about that light switch yourself, and then you take your coat and walk out, leaving the bulb still lit. You go to the park.

Where there are fewer and fewer street lamps as you climb into the big, damp dark. This is the time when everything about sounds like an animal creeping. There will be a sudden hammering burst of tracksuit, jogging and wheezing for health, still too fat to try it in broad day. Make a few tight turns and find a couple, standing noiselessly against each other, so still they have almost disappeared. A blacked-out car passes, looking for a dead end to take.

Once, when the park was like this, you fell into something like love. And then not far from the place where you started, you came back to have the argument that put things to an end. There had been no one you felt like telling about this, so what you said and what you did, how your love was, often seem like no more than imagination now. Only the park can remind you it was real.

One slope which lies behind a flattened stone wall is clear, rough meadow. You have been on this slope in company and now you are alone, but that's alright. From here you can watch down the night to where bridges whip across the river in bright yellow curves and headlamps swing and cut over numb black country hills on the further shore. Closer, you can admire the little golden squares of household light, shining free from towers and blocks and tenement streets that will be grey again tomorrow. Here and now, up on the outside, everyone's life looks pretty good, including yours.

Somewhere to the right below your feet you could, if you wanted, find the single spark of your skylight and perhaps you would notice it flicker every time your father made a leap.

In the morning both your father and mother were at home and kind words heard above the breakfast kettle. No one mentioned the jumping and whenever you crossed beneath the stairwell you avoided looking up. By lunch time Uncle Henry had arrived and was sitting watchfully in the kitchen, facing an opened book.

You were once fond of Uncle Henry, who is your father's brother but really not like him, apart from in the arrangement of his face. When his wife, Aunt Joyce, was still alive you would go and stay with them for weekends and long, peaceful holidays. Uncle Henry was an extremely peaceful man, although this seems more like a kind of tiredness now. In the kitchen with his book, he looked grey. For some reason he had not shaved that day and most of his face was covered with an untidy frost of stubble.

Kneeling behind him in church, you noticed more of the same short and silvery hair at the back of Uncle Henry's neck. It occurred to you that he must sometimes have to shave the back of his neck. Did Aunt Joyce once do that for him? Did a barber take care of him now?

It was terribly sad to see him there, probably praying hard with his head bent and his baby-pink neck flesh exposed. There had been times when he ran in the park with you, faster than you. He was the one to pick you all the way up, one hand fitted neatly under each of your arms and no discomfort or embarrassment between you because he always knew when you would just feel like being taller.

When the time came to learn how to catch and throw things — which seemed important at the time — Uncle Henry was there to help. He was a good man. Even now he will sometimes try to talk to you about your family, about life, about the park, but can't explain what is happening or understand it. You are sure he wants you to be a good person, too, because he thinks you could. Now you are turning out differently, you would rather not speak to him.

Uncle Henry still calls you by your pet name and looks, if you will let him, for a long time, right into your eyes. He tries his best. He can affect you. There are times when you find you have gone to sit in the same room with him, not speaking, and you have come across stupid memories like a drizzly Sunday you both spent in the park. Sliding to a quick stop on a rise of grass Uncle Henry tipped his head full back and left his face completely open to the rain. Water shone all over him and he laughed. You laughed with him and then laughed again when he said, "I love this. There are days when the rain is so good — like we need to be watered."

He slid his thumb down the long dent in his forehead that ran from his hairline to the bridge of his nose. "See that?"

You nodded because you had always seen that, it had been there before you were born.

"That's where they put my head together wrong."

"Who?"

"Whoever made me."

He had been very happy that day. Uncle Henry could often be very happy, it was hard to think why.

Uncle Henry was smiling a little when everyone left the church and eased their weight down into his car. This time he was driving and you had to sit between your mother who was still crying and her mother who was trying to pat at her over your head and hissing words the engine noise made it impossible to hear.

You noticed that other people were now drifting towards the church — it must have been time for a service, for a mass, for something official. In your opinion, the family could have done with something official, rather than being left to its own devices. Your little group had shuffled in and wandered out again without any kind of conclusion being reached; not even a burning candle left behind.

Then again, this hadn't really seemed like a planned visit. You weren't even sure if this had been the family's kind of church, everything had been too urgent for it to matter, like a dash to the Casualty Department or an emergency doctor's call. Your mother had wanted to visit a church and she had wanted a carful of people with her and she wanted to go at once. You don't know why and, when you think, it seems very likely that she doesn't either. That's sad.

The car pulls up at your house and as soon as you can, you get out and very politely you tell anyone who is listening that you are going to take a short walk. They can go inside and set loose whatever is waiting there, it is none of your business now. You are letting it go, putting it out like a cat.

You are heading up the hill, smooth and steady, easing further away from your family and their house. You know the park will be here soon.

RON BUTLIN

I was born in Edinburgh in 1949 then brought up in Hightae, a small village near Dumfries. After leaving school at sixteen, I hitched down to London where I did nothing for a while then secured, in quick succession, the positions of footman, computer operator, translator, and finally the associate member of a rather dismal and forgotten pop group. I wrote song lyrics and, in less than eight months and on the strength of two records and one B-film, retired for good. I went abroad for a while. Returning to Britain, I signed on before becoming a male model, then enrolling as a student at Edinburgh University. Since 1977 I have been a full-time writer with six books and several plays for radio and stage completed to date. At present I am working on a new novel and my second opera libretto.

"Turning Sixteen" is loosely based on my time in London. Like myself at his age, Steve is obsessed about sex. His friend, Chris, seems to be more streetwise and promises to help him meet women. The story is about the relationship — sometimes trusting, sometimes cruel — between them, and how that relationship changes. By the end Steve has a better understanding of sex and of himself. And Chris? I am as unsure now, as I was when I knew him, how confident and experienced he really is.

I enjoy writing short stories like "Turning Sixteen". Even though the events never happened exactly as I write about them, I like to think the stories tell the truth. And if a story has been written honestly, and I did my best, then the reader will be able to share in the truth of what happened.

Remember you are the only person who will ever be you — and using your imagination is the best way of saying how it feels to be you. I scribbled my first poem when I was fourteen — it was terrible. But that didn't matter — the danger is that if you do not at least try, in some way, to say who you are, then even you yourself might never know.

Books by Ron Butlin

Histories of Desire (Bloodaxe)
The Sound of my Voice (Canongate/Paladin/Black Ace)
The Tilting Room (Canongate)
Ragtime in Unfamiliar Bars (Secker and Warburg)
The Exquisite Instrument (Salamander Press)
Creatures Tamed by Cruelty (Edinburgh University SPB)

Turning Sixteen

Two months after running away to London Steve Munro was still a virgin. On the Saturday morning before his sixteenth birthday he lay in bed, thinking. He hadn't even a girlfriend, for goodness sake. Something had to be done — and done today. Someone had to be found, somewhere — in the park, the post office queue, the bus queue, anywhere ... Someone — and before midnight. He was growing older every minute, the days passed too quickly and at night he'd lie awake for hours staring up into the darkness alone and wide awake. He'd only once managed to get a girl into bed, or into a tent to be more exact — Susan. He'd tried sincerity: Let's sleep together, he'd suggested. Be affectionate together. One night's closeness, sharing. She listened. She believed him, she trusted him — and safe in his arms she'd slept. All night. All bloody night while he lay there listening to the rain.

There were ten million people in London — more than twice the population of Scotland — and half of them would be women. Surely just one fancying him out of five million wasn't too much to hope for? Well, here he was. Ready and willing. After midday already — less than twelve hours to go. He was wasting time — he jumped from his bed, washed, dressed and rushed out of his room.

To his surprise, Chris, his flatmate was sitting at the kitchen table finishing a late breakfast.

"Good afternoon, Steve. You take your rest pretty seriously — glued to the sheets were you?" The older boy smiled at him. "Fancy going for a pre-birthday drink and to size up the talent?"

Was the man a mind-reader? "Yeah! Let's go!"

"A moment, young Stephen," Chris raised his hand in mock reproof as he rushed to the door. "The glad-rags first, if you please. Then we go."

Steve came to a sudden halt: "These are my glad-rags."

"Mm," the older boy paused before continuing. "Well, these aren't mine — so if you'd be kind enough to wait a few minutes." He left the kitchen.

Chris had better not take all day to get ready — time was running out. He went over to the window. The older boy would know the best places to go. No problem. He was bound to. Would everything look exactly the same afterwards? The kitchen? The flat? Would he feel different? Be different? There was a mirror in the hall — should he check what he looked like so he'd notice any difference tomorrow? Somewhere out there in London was a girl who, at that very moment, might be brushing her hair, chatting to a friend, doing some shopping ... waiting for him. Less than twelve hours left — why didn't Chris get a move on?

A quarter of an hour later the two of them were walking down Sussex Gardens towards Lancaster Gate. It was a bright windless autumn day. Chris was wearing a dark-blue jacket, a dark-blue tie and white shirt; his trousers were sharply pressed and had turn-ups; his black shoes were highly polished. "Go—" he was saying as he stepped briskly along swinging his umbrella, "that's what it's all about these days. If you don't have go — you'll go nowhere. It's as simple as that," he explained. "For example, take you and me."

No matter how hard Steve tried to keep up, the older boy would walk a little faster so as to set the pace. Maybe to get on down here you had to be a bit of a bastard all the time — Chris certainly was.

"You and me?"

"Well, look at us," Chris remarked turning towards him. "You look —" he paused, considering him closely for several seconds: "Studenty," he said at last.

Did that mean he looked intelligent? An intellectual? His old schoolmates at Dumfries would get a laugh out of that.

"You know — jeans, jersey, that kind of thing," Chris added. "No sense of what's correct or if you fit in. But *me*, on the other hand — well, anyone can see that I'm dressed; that I'm going places. Girls like that. Do you understand?"

Know-all. "I'll get the bus round to Savile Row next payday."

"No need to get shirty!" the older boy joked, adding, "I'm trying to help you, that's all. You're just down from the hills, the frozen north — and it's a different world here. Civilisation, it's called." He smiled, "Don't worry though, you're doing fine. We'll soon have you sorted out, even your accent. Taxi!"

"My accent?" he began, but Chris had stepped forward to secure a taxi that was passing. What was wrong with his accent?

"Greek Street," the older boy curtly ordered the driver when they had taken their seats, then leant forward to slide the glass panel shut. "They're all informers," he explained.

"The drivers?"

"Yes, they listen in on the conversations — that's why I'm being a bit careful." Chris indicated the closed window panel, "Greek Street's in the middle of Soho — the underworld — lots of gangs, drugs, prostitution, protection. He'd have been trying to listen in."

"Is it dangerous then, in Soho?"

"No," Chris answered. "Well, not really."

Not really? What did that mean? He wanted to lose his virginity — not his life.

A short time later the taxi stopped at a street corner and they got out. He tried to pay half the fare but Chris wouldn't let him: "An early birthday present," he was told.

"Thanks very much, that's very kind of you, Chris," he added his companion's name awkwardly, suddenly shy.

"And now," proclaimed his guide once the taxi had driven off, "This is it — all that a man could ask for!"

Steve gazed around him: neon signs proclaimed "Sex", "Hard Core", "Naked Girls" on every side.

"But—" he began. He was wanting a girlfriend, not *this*. The street looked bleak and tatty in the early afternoon light.

Chris wasn't listening. "Nearly two o'clock," he remarked looking at his watch. "Time for a swift one before getting down to business."

The two of them began walking towards a pub at the next corner. As they passed the display window of a strip club, Steve paused to stare in. There was a small hallway inside the entrance of the club, lit by coloured lights: "Adult", "Naked", "Live" — with a velvet-curtained backdrop. A man in a dinner-jacket and bow-tie was chatting to a cashier seated in a small wooden kiosk. Seeing him enter, the man abruptly stopped his conversation and came over.

"In you come, sir. Lovely, lovely girls. The best in Soho — and that's a promise." Then laying a hand on his arm he added confidentially, "Really, sir, a lot of the other clubs round here don't deserve the name: rip-off they are, not strip-off. This is the place." He began leading him towards the cashier.

"Come on, Steve," Chris had grabbed his other arm, "we're not going into this dump."

The doorman ignored the interruption and continued addressing him: "You'll really like Tina, I can tell. *You* could appreciate her, she's got class ..."

Chris jerked him suddenly free of the man's grip and the two of them returned to the street. It must have seemed a bit rude, but the older boy would have known what he was doing.

"Thanks. That's not what I was wanting. Not at all. I ..."

"Too right. You've got to watch yourself, Steve, they're out to bleed you. Pay once at the door, then again inside. Club Membership, they call it," he laughed scornfully. "I'll take you somewhere much better. But first things first," he indicated the pub and the two of them entered.

In Dumfries a pub was usually a place without windows where men stood at the bar drinking until they fell down, were sick, or thrown out — sometimes all three. This Soho pub was luxurious: it had seats, soft lights, a red pile carpet and curtains to match. The bar itself took up only a small part of the room where most of the customers, men and women, sat at low tables talking; music played softly in the background.

"What's yours?" Chris asked hospitably.

"A lager, but you already did the taxi. Let me ..."

The older boy ignored his protests and ordered the drinks.

"Yes, you've got to watch yourself in London. Street life is one thing, but that dump was the gutter: all tease and no strip. No action anyway."

"What kind of place were you thinking of?" Today was going to be the big day all right — Chris seemed to know his way around.

The older boy tapped the side of his nose, "You'll find out, don't worry. Stick with me and you'll have no complaints." The drinks arrived. "Cheers — and Happy Birthday when it comes!" He drank. "Now to business — see anything you fancy?"

Steve glanced round the bar. He was seriously under-age. Could any of these be plain-clothes police? He was in trouble already for running away from home — for one more day anyway. But London seemed full of people that had done the same — at least he'd found a squat to stay in, and a job of sorts at the market.

"Well?"

There were about half a dozen women — none unattached. All of them looked older than he was. One girl, wearing a light summer jacket and jeans, was particularly attractive. He pointed her out.

"She's nice, the one sitting by the door."

"You like them blonde, eh?"

"How do you mean?"

"Well, most people like them either blonde or dark. You know, what you go for in them. So, you prefer blondes?"

"Not all the time."

"The voice of experience, eh!" He paused, then asked, "What've you had so far?"

Nothing. That's what he'd had so far, but he wasn't going to tell Chris.

"Rolling all those Morags and Fionas in the heather!" the older boy laughed. "Drink up, don't look so serious — she's married anyway."

"Married? Who is?"

"The blonde one you fancy, that's sitting with the Escort owner. Hardly speaking so they're bound to be."

"Yeah?"

"Yeah. Sure as it's your round." Chris finished his lager, "I thought you Jocks were big drinkers," and pointed to his half-full glass.

They had just started on their second pint when two girls came in.

"Clocking the new puss?" Chris asked. "Tasty, but I don't fancy yours much."

"Which is mine?"

"Whichever you want — told you I'd see you all right," another knowing tap on the nose. "Cracking stuff round here. Available too, if you know what I mean. That's a woman's greatest asset, her availability."

Steve sipped his drink while glancing over to where the girls were now seated at bar-stools. Really attractive, both of them. Beautiful: one, with long black hair, so dark and mysterious; the other fair-haired, sunny and friendly-looking.

"The two D's," the older boy was saying. "Date them — and dump them. It's the only way," he paused to emphasise his point, taking a sip of lager. "Not forever, of course. A man's got to settle sometime, not yet though," he laughed. "You don't want to be lumbered too soon — or you'll end up like them," with a nod towards the couple still sitting in silence, "*Zomboids* I call that. We're young — time enough for 'mature relationships' when we're good for nothing else."

The dark-looking girl was laughing at something her friend had said. She flicked her long hair back from her face. Had she a boyfriend? He felt a stab of jealousy.

"Which one is it then?"

Was it going to be as easy as that? Chris certainly seemed to know what he was doing. "The one on the left."

"Lady Godiva with the hair, eh? So it's not just blondes. A man of wide tastes," he added. "I'll take Blondie, OK?"

He agreed. Nervously.

"Strategy," announced the older boy. "Let's go." He got to his feet and a moment later had taken up position at a gap in the bar next to where the girls were sitting. Steve picked up his drink and went to join him.

He was close enough now to reach out and touch *her*. Her perfume seemed to fill him, her long hair fell around her. Like darkness. Mysterious — so what could he say to her? How could he even begin? The blonde girl was having difficulties with her cigarette, her lighter wouldn't flame. They were discussing holidays:

"I fancy Greece, but I've never managed it yet," *she* was saying.

"With my compliments to a damsel in distress," Chris interrupted her, smiled, then reached over to the blonde girl with a lighted match that seemed to have appeared from nowhere. Very smooth.

"Thank you," she smiled back.

"No third, or even second light?" the older boy continued. "Does that mean no bad luck for us then?" he asked turning to *her*.

The long-haired girl laughed: "Who knows? Good luck can be when you keep your fingers crossed."

"Well, that's us all right," Chris replied lightly. "It's only nonsmokers who can cross them in the first place." Then, putting down his pint, he crossed his fingers and held them out to show her. She did the same — they both laughed. "Try it," he invited the blonde girl. "And no cheating," he warned as she was about to put down her cigarette.

When she tried and couldn't, the three of them laughed. Steve looked on, and managed to smile. Just. So far he had said nothing and done nothing. What was he — the UN observer? But he'd no idea what to say. He'd crossed his fingers but no one had noticed. Then Chris said "Cheers!" and they all took a sip of their drinks. There was a moment's pause — he should say something now. Before they thought he was deaf or dumb or maybe even both. But what?

"Of course we're all breaking the law here, you know," Chris announced, suddenly gaining both girls' interest once more.

"Breaking the law?" Godiva asked. "Are we?"

"Yes, my friend here especially. He's the master criminal — we're just aiding and abetting."

"Me?" What was Chris on about? He was now the centre of attention. And beginning to go red — he could feel it.

"Yes, ladies. This is a real villain here," the older boy stated with a proprietorial air. "A real villain. Can't you tell by looking at him?"

After a closer inspection — making him even redder — they shook their heads. Godiva had a final stare — as if he was on exhibition.

"Another two years, of course, and no problem. But until then —" Chris made a clicking sound of disapproval, "A criminal, a wanted man."

"Oh, you mean —" he began.

"Anything you say may be written down and used in evidence against you." Chris laughed. The girls thought it was a great joke and laughed again, then looked at him again. He clenched his fists trying not to blush even harder.

"What he means is—"

"Let me introduce to you my flatmate and friend, Steve. Sweet sixteen tomorrow. Another two years, and he'll be old enough to lift a legal pint," he said in a mock whisper. "I'm Chris, by the way."

"Happy Birthday, Steve, when it comes. Cheers." Godiva smiled then made their introductions: *she* was called Claire and her friend was Diane.

He'd get his own back later — for the moment *he* had to say something. Anything. "I heard you talking about Greece, er — Claire. Is it nice?" But she might think he'd been listening to their private conversation. "Or maybe it wasn't Greece? Or—?" he came to a halt.

"You both seem too tanned and body-beautiful for West One," Chris came to his rescue, then grinned: "All-over is it?"

What a question. But the girls just laughed.

Then Claire the dark-haired, the beautiful, turned to him and said, "No, I was saying that I'd like to go there sometime."

"Wouldn't we all!" he replied gaining confidence. "But where have you come back from, being so ..." he hesitated, " ... so tanned?"

"Spain."

"Spain, oh —" He'd never been to Spain — never even been abroad.

"Hardly *real* Spain," interrupted Diane, "Blackpool with sun. Full of English people; Old Brown Cow pubs — even the prices were marked in pounds. I'd spent ages learning up some Spanish phrases for this and that," she continued, turning back to Chris, "and I never even met anyone who spoke Spanish."

"I know just what you mean," Chris said quickly. "I was in a place like that once — went into a taverna and ordered a *cerveza*; the barmaid says, 'A wot?'". He imitated a Cockney accent, "'A wot?'" he repeated laughing.

Both girls laughed. What was a *cerveza*? He tried to catch Claire's eye to smile at her. She looked at her watch.

"Steve was in Spain last year — he was working as a waiter." Chris-the-knowall announced suddenly. "He was just telling me about it."

Claire looked at him: "You were in Spain?" she prompted.

He hesitated: "Mm, yes," he replied. What was he supposed to say?

At that moment "last orders" sounded out. Saved, by the bell.

"That the time?" interrupted Diane. She turned to her friend,

"We'd better run, we're late already."

The two girls immediately finished their wine.

"Goodbye, nice to have met you," Claire added as she got off her stool.

"Goodbye," he and Chris said together.

"Have a good birthday," she called out as she left.

They stood in silence at the bar.

"Couple of scrubbers," Chris said angrily once they'd gone.

"Oh, I wouldn't say—" he protested.

"No, *you* wouldn't say anything. A lot of help you were," came the fierce response. "Let's get out of here."

For the next half hour they trudged around Soho "checking out the action" according to Chris. A bar was pointed out where *gays* met, then where *druggies* met, then *villains*. They were all shut, of course. With the walking and the beer he was beginning to feel tired. An exhaustion that pressed heaviest on his eyes. Just over nine hours left — he didn't intend falling asleep. Nor did he want any more of the guided tour. He yawned.

"Tired? Wanting to go back home, are you?" Chris snapped at him. "Here we are in Soho. I brought you here, at my expense. Be nice to the new guy, I thought, show him a bit of life. Have a few drinks together, then check out the scene — and already you're thinking of giving up," he sneered.

"I never said—"

"What do you want then?"

"Well," he hesitated. "Maybe we could meet a couple of girls and ..."

"'Meet a couple of girls,' he says. A lot of use you were last time."

"I—"

"Of course, we could go to a disco and give the bimbos a thrill. But there's nothing doing with them until you've put a ring on their finger. Waste of time — and money. 'Double rum and coke' are the only words they know." He was angry.

"But—"

"No — you're the birthday-boy. We'll try it your way," Chris insisted in a tone of sudden magnanimity. But the anger was still there.

His way? What was that? At his suggestion they went into the cafe across the road for a rest and a discussion of tactics.

They had been there for several minutes when a large fridge behind the counter switched itself off, and its background hum, which he had not noticed until then, abruptly ceased. He listened but there was only a silence — a sudden emptiness that seemed to grow and cover London then stretch across the whole country, back to Dumfries. Chris resumed talking about blondes and bimbos, the two D's, the same words and phrases repeated over and over again. He stopped paying attention. That silence was echoing inside him now. Tomorrow, he, Steve Munro, would be sixteen.

He sipped his tea and was replacing his cup on the table when all at once it felt as if the schoolboy he had been until a few months ago, and the adult he would become in time, were sitting there with him. His past, present and future — his life. *His*, and no one else's. Briefly, the sense of who he really was seemed to fill the silence that both surrounded and was reaching deep inside him. The girl who was out there somewhere in London also had a past, present and future — a life that was hers alone. He wanted to meet *her* — not just the colour of hair she had; and he wanted her to meet him — not just a lie about working in Spain or an embarrassed lack of conversation. Being *himself* was far more important than whether or not he was a virgin: for when he and she met, their two lives would come together into something quite, quite new.

The silence was fading. Having pushed his cup to one side, Steve interrupted the older boy's monotonous drone before it could overwhelm him once more:

"Thanks for the sights of Soho, Chris, but I'll be off."

"You're leaving? What about the evening puss? There's plenty of places we can still try."

He stood up. "I'm sure there are. But—"

"Chickening out, are you? Not up to it, eh?"

"See you back at the flat."

"Not before morning you won't." Chris tapped the side of his nose. "I'll get on better without you anyway."

It was a bright sunny afternoon when he stepped outside. At the corner, when he turned for a last look down Greek Street, he was just in time to see Chris hesitate outside a strip club and then go in. He shrugged and kept going. He'd go for a walk in Hyde Park — he might even meet Claire. Even if he didn't he would still have his whole life in front of him.